The kiss of death . . .

Sobbing with terror, Elizabeth flung herself into yet another room and slammed the door. There was no place to hide, no place for her to go. From far off in the distance she heard the sound of breaking glass.

Moments later, Nicholas swooped silently into the room. His face was white, except for the warm flush of pink in his cheeks. His cruel, beautiful mouth was carved into a determined smile, and then his hands were on her, crushing her to him.

With all her strength Elizabeth beat against him, screaming. But he subdued her as easily as if she were a dragonfly. Her screams died in her throat as he bent her head back over his arm and slowly sank his teeth into her smooth pale throat.

Bantam Books in the Sweet Valley University series:

SWEET VALLEY UNIVERSITY®

THRILLER EDITION

Kiss of the Vampire

Written by
Laurie John

Created by
FRANCINE PASCAL

BANTAM BOOKS
NEW YORK · TORONTO · LONDON · SYDNEY · AUCKLAND

KISS OF THE VAMPIRE
A BANTAM BOOK : 0 553 50375 8

Originally published in USA by Bantam Books

First publication in Great Britain

PRINTING HISTORY
Bantam edition published 1996

The trademarks "Sweet Valley" and "Sweet Valley University"
are owned by Francine Pascal and are used under license by
Bantam Books and Transworld Publishers Ltd.

Conceived by Francine Pascal

Produced by Daniel Weiss Associates, Inc,
33 West 17th Street, New York, NY 10011

Bantam Books are published by Transworld Publishers Ltd,
61–63 Uxbridge Road, Ealing, London W5 5SA,
in Australia by Transworld Publishers (Australia) Pty Ltd,
15–25 Helles Avenue, Moorebank, NSW 2170,
and in New Zealand by Transworld Publishers (NZ) Ltd,
3 William Pickering Drive, Albany, Auckland.

Printed and bound in Great Britain by
Cox & Wyman Ltd, Reading, Berkshire.

To Taryn Rebecca Adler

Chapter One

"What do you think? Should we put the bar over there?" Elizabeth Wakefield gestured to one end of the ancient, run-down ballroom.

Her twin sister, Jessica, pursed her lips. "I guess so," she said. "You don't think it'll get in the way of people dancing?"

Elizabeth looked around the room again. The rapidly fading mid-October sun was slanting through the dirty windows of the old Hollow House, an abandoned mansion on the edge of the Sweet Valley University campus. It hadn't been lived in for more than twenty years, but it was huge and structurally sound, making it a favorite for university parties.

"Actually, we better allow more room for the band," Elizabeth said. "Let's put the bar at the far end of the dining room, away from the food.

1

Then people will have to mingle." Nodding her head decisively, Elizabeth made some notes on her clipboard.

"Ooh, mingling," Jessica said in a mock-sultry voice. "One of my favorite activities." She flung her long, sun-streaked blond hair dramatically over one shoulder.

Elizabeth looked up and grinned. "In order of importance, does mingling come before or after shopping, gossiping, and blowing off your classes?"

"After shopping, before gossiping, and neck and neck with blowing off my classes," Jessica said thoughtfully.

Elizabeth laughed and handed Jessica the end of a metal tape measure. "Here. Let's see how much room the band will have."

Jessica obediently walked to one end of the room, pulling the tape measure behind her. A sudden gust of wind rattled the unpainted windows in their frames, and Jessica looked up with a little shiver. "Gross weather," she said. "What happened to our beautiful southern-California autumn?"

"This'll pass," Elizabeth said practically. "I bet the night of the Monster Madness party will be gorgeous." The Monster Madness party had been Elizabeth's idea: a huge, all-campus costume party to raise money for Women Against Violence, a local battered-women's shelter. For weeks

2

Elizabeth had been canvassing local businesses, convincing them to donate funds for food, drink, and decorations for the biggest, wildest Halloween party SVU had ever seen. It was scheduled for Friday night, eight days away.

"Thanks for helping me here today, Jess," Elizabeth said, writing down some figures on her clipboard. "I'm supposed to meet soon with the rest of the organization committee. It'll be easier if I have all this information to give them."

"No problem," said Jessica. "The Thetas will eat this up." The Theta Alpha Thetas were considered the best sorority on campus—made up of the most popular, important women at SVU. Jessica had immediately pledged to the Thetas at the beginning of the school year; since then it had been an uphill, clawing climb to maintain her position.

"I wasn't aware that the Thetas liked charity events," Elizabeth said wryly. She walked back through the ballroom and foyer, then into the decrepit front parlor.

It had grown dark outside, and she turned on the electric light. A cobweb-covered chandelier flickered reluctantly to life.

"Are you kidding? The Thetas love to help others," Jessica said, her voice defensive.

Elizabeth raised her eyebrows. "As long as they're helping themselves at the same time."

"Enough, Lizzie. Can't you just appreciate the

fact that I'm hanging out in this dusty old house with you?" Jessica glanced around the room, wrinkling her nose.

Elizabeth gave her twin a smile. When Jessica smiled back, it was like looking in a mirror. Both girls had long blond hair, blue-green eyes, and dimples in their left cheeks. They were the same height, five six, and wore the same size clothes.

But although the exterior packaging was identical, inside, the girls couldn't have been more different. It had been that way since they'd been toddlers. Now that they were college freshmen, their differences had become even more pronounced.

"Well, as long as your motives are in the right place," Elizabeth said finally. "Do you think we should clean this place up a little before the party? Or just leave it as is and call it atmosphere?"

"Call it atmosphere," Jessica said firmly. "It *is* a Halloween party, after all."

"OK." Elizabeth nodded. "Now, as soon as we check the plumbing, we can get going."

"Good. I'm starving."

They went out into the foyer and headed up the wide staircase to the second floor. Faded carpeting was draped limply over the steps, and the banister was strung with spiderwebs. The steps creaked as the girls made their way upstairs.

Jessica giggled nervously. "This is where we

suddenly see the ominous shadow of some creepy guy, and then a crack of lightning splits the sky."

"It's not even raining tonight," Elizabeth pointed out.

On the second floor they checked out the two available bathrooms. Elizabeth made a note to buy some Halloween soap to put next to the sinks.

"So you seeing the Tomster tonight?" Jessica asked. Elizabeth and Tom Watts had been seriously dating for quite a while.

Elizabeth nodded as she wrote. "Yeah. We're kind of in a weird situation. We've both applied for a short internship—we're competing against each other. And we were supposed to get the announcement of who won today. In fact, I've got to go by my mailbox on the way home."

"Huh," Jessica said. "What internship is this?"

"It's really exciting, actually," Elizabeth said. "Have you ever heard of Nicholas des Perdu?"

Jessica shook her head. "Is that his name? Sounds like some kind of gourmet sauce. Like for roasted duck."

"That's his name, all right." Elizabeth left the bathroom and wandered into what must have been a bedroom years before. "He's a world-famous journalist, but he's also incredibly mysterious. Anyway, there was a nationwide competition among journalism majors. The winner gets to fly to New Orleans and meet Mr. des Perdu, and do a

5

two-day research workshop with him. It's a fantastic opportunity. If one of us wins, we'd have to fly out tomorrow afternoon."

"Not much notice. But if it's nationwide, there's no reason to think someone from SVU would win." Jessica airily dismissed the contest. "So—is he cute?"

Elizabeth laughed. "I don't know. I've never seen a picture of him." She walked around the room, looking at the faded wallpaper, now water-stained and peeling, the dirty windows showing black night outside, the carved marble fireplace coated with a thick layer of dust. What kind of person had lived there? Had the room been a woman's bedroom? Someone slept here once, Elizabeth thought—woke here, laughed here, cried here. She shivered.

"Come on—let's go," Elizabeth said. "We're going to miss dinner."

Overhead the electric light suddenly crackled, and the lights flickered out. Instinctively, Elizabeth grabbed Jessica's arm. A blanket of utter darkness dropped over them like cloth.

A second later they were standing huddled together, unable to see even each other's eyes.

"What happened?" Jessica said. Her voice sounded thin and worried.

"I don't know. Maybe the fuses blew," Elizabeth answered. She blinked in the darkness,

6

but her eyes hadn't adjusted yet. Outside, the wind howled, and a nearby crash made them jump. The whole house seemed newly ominous and frightening. Elizabeth struggled to keep a tight grip on her emotions. She had to think clearly. "And that was probably the wind, blowing a shutter closed," she said.

"I want to get out of here." Jessica's grip on Elizabeth's arm was becoming painful.

"OK, OK," Elizabeth said, trying to make her voice sound soothing. "Everything's OK. Oh! Wait—I brought a flashlight!" She pried her arm out of Jessica's grasp to rummage in her backpack. Next to her, Jessica let out a trembly giggle.

"Thank heavens for your Girl Scout training," she said.

Elizabeth flicked the switch on the flashlight, but nothing happened. "I was never a Girl Scout, and you know it."

She tried the switch again and shook the flashlight. Finally a thin, weak beam of pale-yellow light snaked out from her hand.

"I need new batteries," Elizabeth muttered.

"I don't care—let's get out of here," Jessica begged, tugging on Elizabeth's sweater.

Cautiously, Elizabeth led Jessica back to the stairs. The weak beam just barely highlighted the banister a few feet in front of them.

"Careful," Elizabeth said. "Feel with your feet

and hands—don't fall down the stairs." Behind them came the tinkling sound of breaking glass, and both girls tensed.

"Hurry!" Jessica pushed past Elizabeth, then grabbed the banister and practically pulled Elizabeth downstairs.

The hairs on the back of Elizabeth's neck stood up as a cold breeze brushed past them on the stairs. She forced her feet to move as fast as they could without tripping on the worn carpet. The flashlight's pathetic beam wobbled over the ancient stairway.

Normally Elizabeth didn't spook easily, but earlier in the year she had been stalked by William White, a dangerous psychopath who had tried to kill her more than once. Elizabeth knew William was dead and could never hurt her again; still, something inside her had been on edge ever since.

Now she practically jumped the last few steps. Every sound she heard was magnified so that she felt surrounded by a crescendo of banging shutters, howling wind, and whipping leaves. Ahead of her, Jessica's dim outline rushed toward the front door. An odor of dust, faint mildew, and rotting wallpaper swirled around Elizabeth, and she panted for breath.

Jessica flung open the front door and both girls rushed through.

Following an unspoken command, they ran

down the leaf-strewn path as fast as they could. Elizabeth's backpack swung hard against her hip, and the wind whipped her long hair across her face. The chill night air caught in her throat as she struggled to breathe.

They didn't stop running until they reached the campus quad, with its warm streetlights lining the walks.

They slowed, panting, and finally collapsed onto a wooden bench. Elizabeth looked at Jessica sheepishly. "What happened?" she gasped, feeling embarrassed and confused by her reaction to the lights having gone out.

Jessica shook her head. She held one hand to her throat as she drew in deep breaths. "I don't know. I just panicked. I had to get out of there."

"Did we shut the front door?" Elizabeth worried.

"Who cares? There's nothing inside to steal."

Elizabeth sighed, feeling a cool trickle of sweat run down her temple. "I'll have to go back tomorrow and make sure everything's OK."

"Be my guest," Jessica said, standing up and smoothing her jeans over her slim hips. "But count me out. Now, come on, let's go eat. Do you have a brush on you?"

Elizabeth handed her a hairbrush, and Jessica immediately bent over and started untangling her hair.

Frowning, Elizabeth looked back through the

night to where the old Hollow House was hidden behind blackened, overgrown trees. "Yeah. I guess I'll have to go back tomorrow," she murmured.

He opened his front door and took a deep breath. Ah. That wonderful New Orleans air. This time of year it was cool and dense with humidity. He could feel it opening before him, parting to let him through as he made his way to the black wrought-iron gates that led to the street. The evening breeze, scented with late-blooming gardenias and autumn camellias, wafted around him, brushing his cheek with a lover's caress.

It was after midnight. He closed the gate behind him with a smooth, well-oiled click. Out on the street it was impossible to tell that the gates concealed a lush garden, overgrown with writhing vines, gnarled and thickened oak trees of indeterminate age, brick paths slick with green mold.

He adjusted his silk neck scarf and brushed back his smooth black hair with an elegant gesture. The moon was a pale sliver in the cloud-scudded sky; the narrow streets were damp with dew. It was a beautiful night.

He walked several blocks, toward Bourbon Street, which he knew would be crowded and garishly lit, smelling of old beer, stale air-conditioning, and too much cigarette smoke. Fat, middle-aged tourists would be gawking at the swinging doors of the strip joints, where raspy-voiced hawkers promised the thrill of a lifetime. Brash college students would be meandering through the streets of the French Quarter, laughing and shouting. By dawn they would be green-faced, exhausted, and desperate to crawl into their warm, familiar beds.

The images his mind conjured almost made him laugh. Shallow youth. The naïveté. The pointless hope, the unknowing desires, the wasted energy. But youth had its purpose. Sometimes the sight of a young man or woman, poised on the barrier between innocence and knowledge, between anticipation and regret, was enough to make him lose his head, put aside his usual delicate restraints. Sometimes when life offered him such a gift, he just had to take it.

But not tonight. It was too nice a night—too smooth, too mellow, too peaceful. Still, he could imagine the insistent pounding of blood in his ears, feeling another's heart beating frantically against his own, as he used all his powers to subdue, conquer, vanquish. He could almost feel the heady release of yearning.

But no. Tonight was for gentleness, ease, trust. He wanted smiling, generous surrender, an easy glide toward darkness. That was all he was up for.

Turning the corner, he began to make his way toward the river. Already his sensitive nose picked up the scent of the water; curdled, brown, completely opaque, it had been the lifeblood of the city for hundreds of years. He could remember the days before the tankers and the tugboats, when the only sound on the river was the churning of sluggish waves, or the slither of an occasional water snake. Now, of course, it was all different.

For the last few minutes he had been aware, on the dim reaches of his consciousness, of the slight, almost imperceptible sound of another being. There were light footsteps, muffled, feminine, walking ahead of him and to the left. The sound was perhaps two blocks away. He also heard the sharp click of a small dog's nails tapping rhythmically against the sidewalk.

He smiled. His bright-green eyes gleamed with anticipation; his shiny white teeth began to ache deliciously. He felt his energy radiate into the night, searching, searching. *Surrender. You have no choice. Surrender to me now.*

"Let's promise each other that no matter what these envelopes say, we won't let it get between us," Tom Watts said, his dark eyes looking into Elizabeth's. They were each holding a registered letter informing them of the outcome of the internship competition.

Elizabeth nodded. "According to Jessica, neither of us has a chance of winning, anyway. So

12

we can just console each other. If necessary."

Tom rolled his eyes. He piled up a couple of pillows and tucked them beneath his back. He and Elizabeth were propped on opposite ends of his bed, their feet tangled together in the middle. "She has no faith. But I do. And I want you to know that if you win, I'll be happy for you."

"Thanks, Tom." His generosity was only one of the things that made Elizabeth so crazy about him. That and his thick brown hair, dark eyes, and extremely kissable mouth . . . "And if you win, I'll be happy for you," she assured him. Elizabeth reached out and ruffled his hair with one hand.

Immediately his serious expression was replaced by a wolfish gleam. Moving quickly, he bounced to her end of the bed and hugged her tightly. Elizabeth's envelope was tossed aside as Tom pulled her into his arms.

"Tom," Elizabeth murmured as he kissed her neck, her forehead, her nose. "Don't you want to find out about the internship?"

Instead of answering, he kissed her again. Elizabeth wrapped her arms around his neck. For long minutes the only sound in the room was their breathing as it quickened between kisses.

Finally, summoning all her self-control, Elizabeth struggled to a sitting position. She knew her face was flushed and her hair was tangled around her shoulders. Taking a few deep, calming breaths, she tucked in her flannel shirt and fanned her face.

"Elizabeth . . ." Tom clasped her hand, then kissed the palm gently.

"Tom," she mimicked, giving him a warm smile. "When is Danny due back?" she asked pointedly. Danny Wyatt was Tom's roommate and best friend.

Tom groaned and glanced at his clock. "About ten minutes ago," he admitted reluctantly.

Elizabeth quickly redid the barrette in her hair. One of these days she was really going to be embarrassed if Danny barged in on them. It was just hard sometimes: She lived with Jessica, and Tom lived with Danny. They didn't have much time to be alone together.

On the other hand, she mused, feeling the pounding of her heart, maybe that was for the best.

She made sure she'd regained control of her voice. "I'm opening my letter." She picked up the envelope and held it in the air, waving it in front of Tom's face. "You better open yours. . . ."

With a resigned sigh Tom sat up and searched among the bedcovers for his envelope. He found it, somewhat wrinkled, under his blanket. Then, looking into each other's eyes, they ripped the envelopes open at the same time.

It took Elizabeth only a few moments to read what her letter contained. "We're sorry to inform you . . ."

Elizabeth felt her face fall with disappointment. Then she looked up at Tom, who was still silent. "What does yours—"

But she didn't need to ask. It was obvious. Tom's face was lit up, his eyes wide and excited, his lips barely moving as he quickly scanned the rest of the letter.

"I'm really happy for you, Tom," Elizabeth said, laying her hand on his arm. "Congratulations."

He looked up, grinning, then seemed to realize that his success had come at the cost of Elizabeth's rejection. Immediately his face sobered. "I'm really sorry, Elizabeth," he said, gathering her close. "I know how much you wanted that internship."

"No, it's good that you got it," Elizabeth said firmly, pulling away to look at him. "After all, you've got way more broadcast-journalism experience than I do. So did they give you all the details?"

Tom nodded and referred again to the letter. "Yeah. I have to fly to New Orleans tomorrow—my ticket will be at the airline counter. Then in New Orleans someone will pick me up at the airport."

Elizabeth knew he was struggling not to look too excited. She gave him a loud kiss on the cheek. "That sounds wonderful, Tom. And you deserve it. I can't believe you're actually going to meet Nicholas des Perdu."

Tom shrugged modestly, but his face glowed. "It's a great opportunity," he admitted. "I just wish you could go with me. The best thing would be if we could do it together. You deserve it as much as I do."

"Don't worry about me," Elizabeth insisted. "Although I *will* miss you this weekend. But you better start packing if you have to leave tomorrow. What time is the flight?"

"One thirty," Tom answered, checking the letter again.

"OK." Elizabeth put her arms around his waist and kissed him on the mouth. "I'll take you to the airport."

"Thanks, Liz," Tom said, gazing into her eyes. "Your support means everything to me. I couldn't do it without you."

Elizabeth forced herself to grin convincingly. "Just remember that when you win the Pulitzer. I want my name prominently mentioned."

Tom gave her another long kiss. "You got a deal."

Chapter Two

Jessica took another sip of her lukewarm cafeteria coffee on Friday morning, trying to look anywhere but at the two embracing lovebirds across from her. It had been that way all during breakfast, she thought sourly. Elizabeth and Tom, Tom and Elizabeth, gazing sincerely into each other's eyes. It had almost made Jessica lose her appetite. . . .

"I'm going to miss you," Elizabeth murmured across the table.

Jessica took a deep breath and tried not to roll her eyes. After all, she had been known to be lovesick once or twice in her life. *But I was never actually revolting, like this.*

"So, Tom," Jessica said brightly. "What are you going to do in New Orleans? I hear it's a real party town."

Tom tore his attention away from Elizabeth.

"I'm not sure how much free time I'll have," he answered. Looking down, he seemed to realize for the first time that he had a plate of food in front of him. He cut himself a big forkful of pancakes. Elizabeth also busied herself with her breakfast. "It's only a weekend research workshop," she told Jessica. "He might be pretty busy the whole time."

"Oh, he'll have to make time for *some* fun," Jessica said. "I mean, it's a weekend in New Orleans. The city that care forgot."

Tom grinned at her. "You've been reading the brochures."

Jessica shrugged. "I've always wanted to go there. It sounds so old-fashioned and romantic. The plantation houses, the wrought-iron balconies, Mardi Gras . . ."

"The corrupt government, racial tension, high poverty rate, terrible education . . ." Elizabeth baited her.

Jessica tossed her hair over her shoulder. "There's obviously no point in discussing it with you, Ms. Glass-Half-Empty."

Tom held up his hands in a time-out gesture. "Subject change. I'm sorry I'll miss today's planning meeting for the Monster Madness party," he told Elizabeth.

"That's OK," Elizabeth assured him. "At least you'll be here for the actual party. Have you been thinking about your costume?"

18

"I think we should go as a pair." He swallowed his last bite of pancakes. "I could be Frankenstein, and you could be my bride. Or I could go as a vampire, with you as my victim."

"Isn't that sort of sexist?" Jessica said.

"Jessica's right," Elizabeth said indignantly. "Why can't I be the vampire and you be the victim?"

"Or you can be Frankenstein and he can be the bride," Jessica added with a smirk.

"Fine." Tom held up his hands in defeat. "I'm just saying I thought it would be fun to coordinate what we wear. That's all."

"Yeah. You guys could go as peanut butter and jelly," Jessica said. "Or as Mickey Mouse and Minnie. Or Scarlett and Rhett. Or Commander Riker and Counselor Troi."

"They broke up," Tom pointed out.

Jessica shrugged. "Whatever."

"What are you going to be?" Elizabeth asked Jessica.

"Catwoman," Jessica said, narrowing her eyes in pleased anticipation. She had her costume all planned: a shiny black bodysuit, high, pointy-heeled boots, and a cute little hood with cat ears standing straight up. Half the guys at the Monster Madness party would be drooling. The other half would be falling all over themselves trying to get to her.

"How . . . appropriate," Tom said with a straight face.

Elizabeth punched him in the arm. "That sounds great, Jess," she said.

"Of course it does." Jessica finished her coffee and looked at her watch. "If memory serves, I have a class soon. Tom, have a great trip. You'll be back Sunday, right?"

"Right. Have a good weekend, Jessica." Tom looked at his watch, too. "I better get going. Last-minute stuff."

"OK," said Elizabeth. "I'll come pick you up at twelve thirty."

"Great."

Jessica tried not to watch as Tom leaned over and kissed Elizabeth lingeringly. *Geez. In a public place. Who would have guessed that my boring sister would turn out to be almost as passionate as I am?*

At twelve thirty on the dot, Elizabeth pulled up outside Tom's dorm in the black Jeep that she and Jessica shared. There was a weight on her chest that she couldn't shake off.

I'm not really jealous of Tom, am I? she wondered. *Of course I want him to do well.* Sighing, she honked the horn a couple of times. In less than a minute Tom came bounding out of his dorm, a green canvas duffel bag flung over his shoulder.

"Hi, Liz," he said, giving her a kiss. He tossed the duffel bag into the back and swung up into the passenger seat. "I really appreciate the ride to the airport," he told her as he snapped his seat belt shut.

"I'm happy to do it." She started the Jeep and pulled out of her parking space. "Are you sure you have everything?"

"I think so. Paper, pens, laptop. Clothes. Toothbrush. Anything I forgot, I can buy. I have to tell you—I'm pretty nervous about meeting Nicholas des Perdu. I wish I had at least talked to him before, or something."

Elizabeth gave Tom a thoughtful glance. He was usually pretty confident. If he was having second thoughts about this internship, she hoped it wasn't for her sake.

"He sounds totally fascinating," Elizabeth said. "Isn't he supposed to be pretty young? He's accomplished so much in a short time. I know you're going to get a lot out of it." Despite her reassuring words, again Elizabeth felt a pang of depression, tinged with unease. She almost wished that Tom wouldn't go. That somehow something would happen so that he *couldn't* go. *Elizabeth, stop it,* she scolded herself.

"I guess I will," Tom said. "I don't even know what he's working on—what research I'll be doing. But I'll see New Orleans. That's something."

"Tom, this is a great opportunity," Elizabeth said brightly. "I know you'll have an incredible time." She bit her lip to keep it from trembling.

"You're right," Tom said, looking out the

Jeep's window as the airport came into sight. "It's going to be great. But I'll miss you. I'll call as soon as I get in, OK?"

"You better," Elizabeth responded, forcing herself to smile.

As promised, Tom's ticket was waiting at the airline counter. Elizabeth walked with him through the metal detectors and then on to his gate, where the first-class passengers of his flight were already boarding.

Dropping his bag at his feet, Tom took Elizabeth's face between his hands. He bent down and kissed her tenderly, as though they would be separated for years instead days. "I'll miss you," he whispered.

"I'll miss you, too," Elizabeth whispered back. She gazed into his dark eyes as if trying to memorize every detail of his face. "Oh—that reminds me." Feeling a little embarrassed, she unzipped her purse and pulled out a heavy white envelope. She handed it to Tom.

A warm smile crinkled the edges of his eyes and turned up the corners of his mouth as he opened the package and pulled out its contents. "It's beautiful," he said. "Just what I needed."

Elizabeth wasn't sure why she'd felt compelled to give him this picture of herself—it had just seemed like a good idea that morning, when she'd been restlessly prowling her room after breakfast.

The black-and-white photo wasn't recent, and Elizabeth wasn't smiling, wasn't even looking at the camera. Instead, her eyes were focused wistfully on some far-off point beyond the camera's range. She had got the pretty inlaid wooden frame at a stationery shop.

Tom carefully tucked the picture into his duffel bag, then kissed Elizabeth again. "Thanks," he said. "I know I'll feel at home when I put your picture next to my bed."

When Tom's row number was called to board, Elizabeth pulled him to her for one last kiss. With a final wave he disappeared down the long hallway that led onto the plane.

A few minutes later Elizabeth stood pressed against the plate-glass window, watching as the plane taxied down the runway and finally took off. She watched it until it was just a bird-sized speck in the clear blue sky, taking Tom away from her.

Ah, Friday afternoon, Jessica thought happily, wiggling her toes. She was lying on an elegant chintz couch in the Theta living room, her shoes kicked off. She was enjoying the fact that her classes ended early on Fridays; now she was free, free, free until Monday morning at ten thirty. Well, free except for a couple of annoying reports and tests coming up. The usual school stuff. College would be vastly improved, in Jessica's opinion, if there weren't so many academic requirements involved.

In the kitchen she could hear Lila Fowler and a couple other Thetas fixing afternoon tea. *What a civilized ritual,* Jessica thought. Just another indication that the Thetas were the best. But then, she had always known that. Alice Wakefield, the twins' mother, had been a Theta years before, when she had attended SVU.

"Hey, Jess." Lila came in and plopped down in a chair across from Jessica. Her long light-brown hair was held back in a heavy gold barrette, and she was wearing fine wool stirrup pants, a cream cashmere turtleneck, and a tweedy melton blazer. As usual, she was the epitome of modern, expensive good taste. "What are you reading?"

Jessica held up her copy of *Cosmo*. "Tea almost ready?"

Lila nodded. "Maybe we should make a fire. It's down to almost seventy degrees outside."

"Ooh. Break out the fake-fur coats," Jessica said with a grin. "These brutal California autumns."

Lila grinned back at her, and for a few moments they sat in companionable silence. Jessica and Lila had been best friends off and on—mostly on—since second grade. No one, except maybe Elizabeth, really understood Jessica the way Lila did. But there was an adversarial quality to their friendship, too. The two girls also enjoyed an ongoing friendly competition, and after ten years they knew what to expect from each other.

"Seeing Randy tonight?" Lila asked as another freshman Theta pledge brought in the tea tray.

Jessica sat up expectantly, already eyeing the delicate cucumber sandwiches, the thinly sliced pound cake, and the petits fours. She nodded her head. "Yep. New movie at the Odeon."

Randy Mason was Jessica's latest boyfriend. He was an all-around nice guy, and he was a lot of fun. After spending the first few months of her freshman year on an emotional roller coaster, Jessica was relieved to be dating someone who was wonderfully uncomplicated.

Smiling at the thought of her date with Randy, Jessica helped herself to a bone-china cup and saucer and filled the cup with fragrant, steaming Earl Grey. "And you?" she asked Lila. Taking a sip of hot tea, she batted her eyelashes innocently.

"Yes, I'm seeing Bruce tonight," Lila said with just the faintest touch of blush rising in her cheeks.

Bruce Patman was a sophomore whom Lila and Jessica had known since grade school. For the last ten years he had been simultaneously utterly obnoxious and completely adorable; both a bane of their existences and a darkly attractive romantic possibility. Jessica had been involved with him briefly back in high school and considered her timely escape lucky. But Lila had recently decided that there was more to Bruce than snide insinuations, lewd innuendos, and arrogant good looks. Jessica still thought Bruce was a jerk, but she got a perverse kick out of seeing Lila so in love with him.

"Good. It's always best to keep it in the family, dear," Jessica said wryly, referring to the fact that the Fowlers and the Patmans together represented most of the significant wealth of Sweet Valley.

Lila raised her eyebrows. "If you gave him half a chance, you'd realize that there's more to Bruce than money."

The Theta front door closed gently, and Magda Helperin, Theta president, and Alison Quinn, Theta vice president and snake extraordinaire, came in. As usual, they were both impeccably well-groomed.

"Hi, Magda," Jessica said. "You're just in time for tea." She ignored Alison.

"Great," Magda said. "Are any other sisters around?"

Lila nodded. "Yeah—we pretty much have a full house this afternoon." Although Lila lived in a dormitory, Jessica knew she considered the Theta house her home away from home.

"Good," Magda said, taking off her navy blazer and draping it gracefully over the back of a wing chair. "I have some news to share with all of you. Alison, could you please round up everyone in the house?"

"Sure." Not sparing Jessica a glance, Alison headed up the carpeted stairs. Moments later they heard her voice in the hall, calling an informal Theta meeting.

Soon there were about ten Thetas gathered in the living room around the fire that had just been lit. Tea was poured, sandwiches were passed, greetings were exchanged. It was a comfortable, homey scene, and it made Jessica writhe with impatience.

Get on with your news already. She sent the mental message to Magda. What was she waiting for?

Magda leaned back on the couch and sipped her tea. "This is just a very casual get-together," she said, meeting eyes with everyone in the natural-leader way she had. "And it won't affect most of you at all. But I wanted everyone to know what was going on at one time, just to be more efficient."

Jessica glanced around the room. There were a few Thetas missing, but in general, the sorority was well represented. This one room held the most important and sought-after women on campus. Each one had fresh, natural good looks and charisma. Each was dressed well, from the very conservative president to Lila's flashier, expensive look, to Jessica's tight black miniskirt. Jessica felt incredibly proud to be part of such a prestigious organization.

"It's not a big deal, really," Magda continued with

a shrug. "Basically I wanted to announce that we're turning the back parlor into a bedroom, and it will be available to any Theta without her own room now."

Jessica's eyes widened with anticipation. An available bedroom! It was what she'd been waiting for. Living with Elizabeth in Dickenson Hall had been bearable, but anyone with half a brain would rather have her own room at the Theta house. No contest.

"I know most of you are happy where you are," Magda said. "But Alison has mentioned that she wouldn't mind a different room, and I know Jessica has been wanting to be more integrated in Theta life." Magda paused to smile at each of the girls. Jessica tried to look worthy without seeming too greedy.

"So—the room is available. I've decided it wouldn't be fair for me to arbitrarily assign the room, so anyone who's interested will have to work it out with your sorority sisters. I know you'll be generous and thoughtful in this." She smiled benevolently. "That's it—meeting adjourned."

One by one, the Thetas headed back to their rooms, or to the kitchen, or out to the library, or to do errands. After a few minutes only Jessica, Alison, and Lila remained in the living room.

"You can forget it, Jessica," Alison said in a bored tone. "I have seniority on you, and I'm vice president. Of course the room is mine." She examined her fingernails with interest.

Alison and Jessica had never got along. And ever since Alison had tried to get Jessica blackballed from the sorority, the girls had been archenemies.

"Funny, that's not what I heard Magda say," Jessica countered. "In front of witnesses, too. I believe the room is up for grabs. *You* might as well give up now."

"Jessica, you're only a freshman," Alison pointed out, making the word sound like an incurable disease.

"And you're only a lying, cheating snob," Jessica said back in a singsong voice. "Don't waste your time pretending the room is yours. I want it, and I'm going to have it."

Alison's cold gray eyes burned with anger. She stood up, her hands clenched into fists at her sides. "Don't bet on it," she spit out, then turned and stomped upstairs to her old room.

Jessica made a face at Lila, who had been watching their squabble with interest.

"Don't bet on it," Jessica mimicked in a high-pitched voice. "*That* was a stinging comeback. That really put me in my place. Oooh—'Don't bet on it.' I'm scared now."

In her armchair, Lila giggled. "If I were you, I'd start watching my back."

"Lila," Jessica said indignantly, "I *always* watch my back."

Chapter
Three

"Ladies and gentlemen, welcome to the Crescent City. Please remain in your seats until the captain has turned off the seat-belt sign."

Tom checked his watch. Back in Sweet Valley, it was about four thirty in the afternoon. Here, central standard time put him at about six thirty. The late-October sun had already set.

Once he had gathered his duffel bag and made his way into the airport terminal, Tom was struck by how much a public building could impart the personality of a city. The Sweet Valley airport was new, bright, and clean—with pastel colors, fresh-juice bars, and lots of indoor plants. The New Orleans airport looked older, a bit darker, and less modern. The air was heavy, moist, and smelled faintly of mildew.

Tom's letter of acceptance had stated that

someone would pick him up at the main airport entrance at seven. Glancing at his watch, Tom realized his plane must have been a few minutes early.

He bought a newspaper, and a minute later he was leaning against a fire hydrant outside the airport, scanning the headlines on the front page. The air was positively muggy and warm, and Tom loosened his tie and unbuttoned his jacket. People streamed around him, heading for the parking lots, and Tom felt a quick rush of excitement.

Here he was, in New Orleans. He was on a professional assignment as a journalist, more or less. After he graduated, he would be doing this kind of thing all the time—he'd fly all over the world, maybe even into wartime situations, covering important stories . . . and this was his start, his big break. Two days with a man who was famous for doing exactly what Tom wanted to do.

Impatient for his ride to arrive, Tom read through a couple of articles. As he'd expected, the paper covered mostly local news. Scandals about casino gambling, the New Orleans Saints lost to the Miami Dolphins . . . woman dead by exsanguination . . .

Exsanguination? What's that?

His perusal of the article was interrupted by the arrival of a sleek black limousine pulling up in front of him. A nondescript white man wearing a chauffeur's uniform got out and smiled at Tom.

31

"Tom Watts? I'm Fortune. Mr. des Perdu sent me for you. I hope you haven't been waiting long."

"No, not at all." Tom smiled back as Mr. Fortune took his one duffel bag and locked it in the trunk.

When the driver opened the back door for Tom and indicated that he get in, Tom felt almost like a fraud. People were looking at him, wondering if he was important or famous. As the limo drove away into the black night, away from the bright airport lights, Tom sank back into the leather upholstery. *I have a feeling this trip is going to change my life.*

Tom, are you thinking about me? Elizabeth gazed at the picture of him she kept on her desk. *I'm thinking about you.* Without even trying she remembered the feel of his arms around her, his mouth on hers . . .

Shaking her head, she willed herself to break out of the vague sense of melancholy that had been plaguing her all day. It was barely five o'clock—he might not have even arrived in New Orleans yet.

Snap out of it, she commanded herself. With a renewed sense of purpose, she clicked on her desk light and applied herself to her communications textbook. After all, Tom would be gone for a weekend. It's not as if she were some spineless sap who couldn't function without her boyfriend around. Absolutely not. She was Elizabeth Wakefield, strong and self-sufficient.

After her high-school boyfriend, Todd Wilkins, had unceremoniously dumped her at the beginning of the school year, she had been devastated. That experience had made her swear that she would never depend on a guy to make herself feel complete. While Tom was away, she would use the time productively to catch up on her schoolwork, put in extra hours at WSVU, see all her friends, do laundry . . .

"Oh! You will not believe this!" Jessica's outraged voice broke into Elizabeth's thoughts just as the door to their room banged open and crashed against Elizabeth's closet.

"What is it?" Elizabeth looked at her sister mildly. When Jessica made an announcement like that, she never knew what revelation was going to follow. The problem might be an extra-long nail that had suddenly snapped off, or she might have just got kicked out of SVU for flunking all her classes.

Jessica began to stalk angrily up and down their small room. "This is just unbelievable," she said. "Lizzie, I'm going to need your help."

Elizabeth waited patiently for Jessica to continue. Finally Jessica sat down on Elizabeth's bed with a loud sigh. "There's a bedroom opening up at the Theta house. A fabulous private bedroom on the first floor."

"And?" Elizabeth prompted.

"And I want it! Duh. Haven't you been listening?" Jessica looked at her accusingly. "The only problem is Alison Quinn. She wants it, too."

"You want to move into the Theta house?" Elizabeth wasn't surprised, exactly. Practically the first week of school Jessica had bailed on Elizabeth to room with Isabella Ricci, her new best friend after Lila. Then Jessica had moved in with Mike McAllery, a guy she'd fallen head over heels in love with for a short, but eventful, time. Now, when it felt as if things were more or less settled into normalcy, Jessica was jumping ship again.

"Of course I do," Jessica said with a frown. Then she looked up at Elizabeth, her eyes softening. "Look, Liz, it's not like I don't *like* living here. But I've been hoping to get a room in the Theta house all year. And face it—we're both better off if I have a room to myself." She glanced meaningfully around the dorm cubicle they called home.

As usual, Elizabeth's side was perfectly neat, everything put away, drawers closed, textbooks stacked, CDs in their holder. Jessica's side looked like the aftermath of a 7.8 on the Richter scale.

Elizabeth couldn't help smiling. "Oh, I don't know, Jess. Ever since I got the snow shovel, I haven't had any trouble finding my bed."

Jessica made a wry face. "Are you going to help me or not?"

"How can I help? I don't have anything to do with the Thetas. Anyway, what does Magda say? She's the president. What she says goes."

"She says we have to work it out among ourselves," Jessica groaned, flopping backward. "And when you're talking about me and Alison, that means a fight to the death."

"Hmm." Elizabeth leaned back in her desk chair and stretched her arms over her head. "What if Alison got the new room, and you got her old room?"

"First of all, I don't want to give Alison the satisfaction of getting what she wants. That witch spent months making my life miserable. I'm not about to do her any favors." Jessica sat up again. "Besides, Alison already shares with another junior. The downstairs room is *private*. It's a *single*. I *have* to have it."

"But how can I help?" Elizabeth repeated.

"I don't know," Jessica admitted, sitting up and swinging her legs over the side of the bed. "I just want to make sure you're on my side. This could get bloody."

"Jessica. You're my twin. Have I ever not been on your side?"

"Mr. Fortune?"
"Just Fortune, Mr. Watts."

"Oh. OK. Um, you know, I haven't seen a single hill or mountain or anything. Is New Orleans really this flat, or does it just look that way because it's dark?"

In the rearview mirror Tom could see Fortune smile. "It's really this flat, Mr. Watts," the driver said. "Most of what we're driving through is reclaimed swampland."

"Oh. How far away is Mr. des Perdu's house?"

"Not far now. He lives in the French Quarter. You've heard of the Quarter?"

"Yes, and I've always wanted to visit. Hey, what's that place, on the left?" Out the window Tom could see what looked like acres of little white cement huts. A tall wrought-iron fence with spikes surrounded it. It looked like some primitive village for very small people.

"That's the St. Louis Cemetery," Fortune replied.

"A cemetery? What were all those little buildings?"

"They're mausoleums. Each family has their own. When someone dies, they open up the family crypt and push the new coffin in. Older coffins get dropped down to the bottom," Fortune explained.

Tom frowned. "People aren't buried in the ground?"

Again Fortune smiled in the rearview mirror. "New Orleans is five feet below sea level," he said. "The water table is barely below the surface of the ground. If you bury a coffin in the earth, the next time it rains, it pops right back up again." When Fortune grinned, Tom could see a gold tooth set far back in his mouth.

An unbidden image of a coffin smeared with a thick layer of mud came to Tom's mind. He pushed the mental picture away. Then he leaned forward in anticipation as the long dark car turned into a narrow street. Old-fashioned streetlamps showed two- and three-story stucco houses lining both sides of the street. Several of them were painted pink or peach or other pastel shades. Narrow balconies, hung with intricate wrought-iron scrollwork, overlooked the street.

Tom rolled down his window to get a better view and was immediately assaulted by a rolling wave of dense, wet air. It smelled amazingly different from the air in California—sweet, yet somehow not fresh. Warm. Seductive.

Tom laughed a little to himself. He was already falling under the spell of the city.

Then Fortune turned into a pair of tall, narrow gates. A few moments later a house came into view. Tom climbed out of the limo, drinking in his first sight of the home of Nicholas des Perdu.

"It's like something out of a movie," he breathed, hardly aware that he had spoken aloud. But Fortune, walking toward the house with Tom's duffel, nodded.

"Yes," he said. "Nothing about the house belongs in the twentieth century."

The walk leading to the house was made of soft red brick, and it felt damp and slimy beneath Tom's loafers. The garden, if it could be called that, was overgrown. The plants were wild and untamed, and Tom loved their lushness. He felt drawn toward the plants that seemed to have a will of their own.

Tom shook his head as if to clear it. What was wrong with him? He felt as though he'd walked onto another planet; Sweet Valley seemed a million light-years away. It wasn't like him to be so susceptible to atmosphere. Maybe the flight had tired him more than he'd thought.

The building itself looked like Tom's idea of a plantation house. It was hard to believe that the mansion was right in the middle of downtown New Orleans. Two stories high, its white paint gently peeling, the house stood in the middle of the green lawn and garden with an air of well-bred decay. Each floor was lined with tall French windows. Tom gazed at the house, wondering about its history.

Though the autumn air was soft and warm, he found himself shivering.

Chapter Four

Fifteen minutes later Tom was surveying his room. It was on the second floor, and its glass doors led to a balcony. The windows were open, and their sheer curtains gently billowed in the breeze.

Tom looked around uncertainly. Fortune had left him at the front door, and then an amazingly pretty young housekeeper named Marielle had shown him to his room.

"Nicholas will be right with you," she'd said in a slightly husky voice that Tom was uncomfortably aware he found sexy. "Just make yourself at home—as if you were never going to leave."

"Thanks," Tom muttered in confusion.

With a small smile Marielle had closed the door behind her, leaving Tom alone.

The room was large and filled with antiques. Tom's family home hadn't had any antiques. His mother had preferred fresh, light furniture in pale shades; their house had looked almost like a beach house, a summer home. This house, Nicholas's house, looked old-fashioned and untouched. It was as if no one had bothered to change anything for hundreds of years.

Tom checked his watch. Almost eight o'clock. He'd eaten on the plane, so he wasn't hungry—but he was starting to wonder where his host was. He felt strange being left alone in this room, unsure of what to do. Should he try to find Mr. des Perdu? Feeling a touch of uneasiness, Tom emptied his duffel. He set his laptop computer and notebooks on the desk, then dumped his clothes into the huge marble-topped chest of drawers.

When his fingers touched the smooth wooden frame of Elizabeth's picture, he smiled. Taking it out of his bag, he studied it closely. Her face was so familiar, so loved. There was the beauty of her almond-shaped, blue-green eyes, the curve of her cheekbone, her soft mouth. An unexpected dull ache settled in his chest. What was he doing there? How had he been able to leave her so easily? For one second he would have given anything to be back in comfortable Sweet Valley, holding Elizabeth tight, breathing in her scent.

But he was here, in a strange city, in a strange house, more than a thousand miles away. And he had a job to do. After trailing his finger lightly down Elizabeth's cheek, he set the picture on his bedside table.

"Hello, Mr. Watts."

Whirling in surprise, Tom found himself looking into startling bright-green eyes.

"I am Nicholas des Perdu," the man said smoothly. "I'm sorry if I startled you. I tapped on your door, but there was no answer."

"Oh, no problem, Mr. des Perdu," Tom stammered. Pulling himself together, he took a couple of small steps and grasped his host's hand. He had to look professional. He had to look worthy of this internship. After all, he had been chosen out of more than a hundred applicants, nationwide.

"Please, call me Nicholas," the older man said with an easy smile. Actually, Tom realized after a second glance, des Perdu didn't look that much older than he. The man was tall and slender, though Tom detected a wiry strength hidden beneath Nicholas's expensive, almost formal clothes. His skin was pale—surprisingly pale; his eyes were the bright green of a glass bottle. His longish black hair was combed straight back off his aristocratic forehead. Tom guessed that most women would find him compellingly attractive.

"OK, thanks—Nicholas," said Tom. "And I'm—Tom." He felt foolish as soon as the words were out of his mouth. Obviously, a wealthy, world-famous journalist didn't need Tom's permission to use his first name. To cover his discomfort, Tom stuck his hands into his pockets. *The guy's hand is like ice,* he noted silently. *Hard to manage that in this climate.*

"How was your flight?" Nicholas continued, seemingly unaware of Tom's feelings of awkwardness. He settled himself in a comfortable chair next to the desk, his long limbs folding effortlessly into place.

"Fine, fine," Tom said. "I wish I could have seen more of New Orleans on the drive from the airport. Maybe tomorrow, during the daytime."

"Yes, of course you must do some sight-seeing tomorrow. This is one of the most beautiful and individual cities in America. Though I personally find New Orleans at her most seductive at night." When Nicholas smiled, his pearly white teeth against his ashen skin were almost shocking. Tom felt himself drifting off balance. "New Orleans is like a woman," Nicholas went on softly, staring at Tom. "Only under the cloak of night can she be coaxed to reveal all her secrets."

Tom's grin was frozen into place. He had never met anyone who talked this way, and he had no idea how to respond.

"So!" Tom said finally, feeling desperate to change the subject. "I'm really excited about this internship. I've been a big fan of yours for a long time. The series of articles you did about the Soviet Union's breakup was fascinating."

Nicholas smiled again, and Tom felt himself warming to him. He seemed like a nice guy—a little odd, maybe, but then, he was brilliant. Lots of brilliant people were eccentric. Tom pulled up a straight-backed chair and sat near Nicholas.

"Thank you," Nicholas said. "How flattering, especially coming from such a gifted student of journalism. Now I'll tell you a bit about my—our—current project. Basically, it has to do with Halloween in New Orleans. The holiday here has a very different feel than it does, say, in Salem, Massachusetts, or in New Mexico, where it's been strongly influenced by the Mexican Day of the Dead celebration." He paused while Tom quickly flipped open his notebook and began writing. "Here the holiday has strong religious overtones—New Orleans is a very Catholic city, if you didn't know. And, of course, the day after Halloween—All Saints' Day—is in some ways the more important festival."

"All Saints' Day?" Tom asked, writing it down. "What's that?" Already he was excited about the research project ahead of him. Halloween had always been just Halloween to him. The idea that it served different needs for different cultures was fascinating.

Nicholas put his long, slender white fingers together. His hair, so black that it seemed to absorb light, waved back from his temples like wings. He was the most charismatic person Tom had ever met.

"All Saints' Day follows Halloween, and most

schools and businesses are closed for holiday. It is a day for remembrance, a day to honor those who are no longer with us." His eyes, a green so pure they reminded Tom of a cool mountain stream, seemed to penetrate Tom's skull. "On All Saints' Day families across the city visit their ancestral tombs," Nicholas explained. "Traditionally, it is the day one paints, makes repairs, puts out fresh flowers, lights candles. . . . It is somehow special, is it not, to set aside a whole day to do nothing but remember those we have lost? So civilized."

Lost in Nicholas's voice, Tom could only nod. Listening to his host was like watching sharks swim in tanks—it was hypnotic. There was something unusual about his voice, Tom thought. It sounded almost as if English was his second language. He spoke it perfectly, with no trace of an accent, but there was a precision, a crispness, to his consonants that hinted of another language spoken a long time ago.

With an effort Tom pulled his mind back to the present and reviewed his notes. "That's incredibly interesting, Nicholas. I can't wait to get started. What exactly can I help you with?" When there was no answer, Tom looked up.

Across from him, Nicholas was frozen in his seat, his emerald gaze locked on something beyond Tom's head. Tom turned, half expecting to see something sneaking up on him, but saw nothing. "Nicholas?"

There was no response, and his host's intense focus didn't waver. Tom turned around again, then looked back at Nicholas. It almost appeared as if Nicholas was looking at Elizabeth's picture on Tom's bedside table. Was he? Tom double-checked. Yes, the man was positively staring at it. Tom frowned.

Lisette. Nicholas felt as if he'd suddenly been thrown more than two hundred years into the past. *It is Lisette.* But it was impossible—Lisette had been dead since 1789. How was it that her face, more familiar to him than his own, could appear in a modern photograph?

Nicholas could see her, still conjure her image as if she yet lived and breathed by his side. . . .

. . . The large Gothic cathedral was splashed with bright, gaily colored light from where the autumn sun pierced the stained-glass windows.

October 31, 1788. A good day for a wedding.

The smoke from holy incense filled the air and tickled Nicholas's nose, forming a haze over the marble altar, and swirling opaque halos around the plaster figures of patron saints. Nicholas was aware of his family's impatience and concern, but he tried not to let it show on his face.

Lisette, I know you're coming. Are you in danger?

Several feet from him, the bishop of Paris shifted his weight from foot to foot. His chasuble, heavily em-

broidered with gold thread and encrusted with jewels, rustled softly. Nicholas refused to look at him. Was Lisette safe? The streets of Paris were so uncertain these days. . . . Inside the cathedral the air was heavy and still, but sounds of the ever-present dissension, of panic, of anger filtered through the heavy wooden doors.

Fool! Why did you not send your own guards to escort her?

In the countryside, Nicholas knew, people were starving. The manager of his own property had sent unbelievable reports, reports that would make a lesser man panic. But Nicholas had always lived in Paris—he had little to do with running the family estate. He didn't put faith in the almost hysterical messages his overseer had been sending. And yet here in the very streets of his beloved city, he saw more and more people swarming, protesting, marching. It was all so unpleasant.

Once again the small group of musicians seated high in the choir balcony above the church began to repeat their repertoire.

It had been nearly two years since he had first seen Lisette, first looked into her eyes and saw his salvation. She had been barely fifteen, while he'd been almost twenty-three. In the two years since, the charming schoolgirl on the verge of beauty had ripened into the fulfillment of womanly promise. Her sweet, unmolded face had matured into an exquisite

46

sculpture. Her giggly, self-conscious personality had been tempered into a graceful strength, modest and determined at the same time. And she had determined to have Nicholas, just as he had determined to have her.

Nicholas's head snapped around as the heavy wooden doors to the cathedral were flung open. The group of family, friends, and professional celebrants jerked with surprise. Nicholas tensed, his hand automatically going to the sword at his side.

A small figure, wearing the private colors of the duc de Chavonne, stood surrounded by guards at the doorway.

Lisette. My love. I knew you would come.

She was dressed in billows of icy-blue silk, her long skirt brushing the inlaid marble parquetry of the floor. Lacy cuffs at her wrists encircled the small posy of lilies of the valley that she carried. A sheer scarf of the finest pale-blue organdy, shot through with silver threads, was draped over her head and shoulders, concealing her face. Slowly, with measured steps, Lisette, the love of Nicholas's life, began her procession up the aisle of the cathedral.

Nicholas could feel himself tremble. At last the moment had come. Tonight Lisette would be his, and he would be hers, for all eternity. She stopped when she reached the altar, then placed her tender hand in his. He could feel the light, fluttery beat of her pulse, as if his hand held a small wild bird.

As the bishop spoke the words uniting them before the eyes of God and man, Nicholas wondered dumbly what he had done to deserve such a gift. There was no doubt Lisette was an angel sent from heaven to rescue him from misery, to give purpose to his pathetic existence. She shed radiant joy on a life that had been cast of the dullest lead.

And now she was his bride.

With trembling fingers Nicholas lifted the edge of the veil and raised it over Lisette's head. Her almond-shaped blue-green eyes, shining with happiness, gazed into his. Nicholas gently traced the curve of her cheekbone, the fullness of her mouth. Her golden hair, streaked with strands of moonlight and sunlight, brushed his fingertips as he lowered his mouth to hers.

"Mr. des Perdu? Nicholas?" *What in the world is wrong with him?* Tom wondered. He hoped Nicholas wasn't sick, or in some weird fugue state.

Suddenly Nicholas's stare snapped back to Tom's face. He shook his head slightly. When he smiled, it seemed strained. "Forgive me," he said in his melodious voice. "I lost myself for a moment."

Tom glanced back at Elizabeth's picture, then at Nicholas.

"Where were we?" Nicholas began almost briskly, looking down at his hands. "Oh, yes. Your research. What I would like you to do is—"

"That's my girlfriend, Elizabeth," Tom said, surprising himself by interrupting Nicholas.

"Oh?" Nicholas gave him a polite, detached smile. "You left her behind in Sweet Valley, I take it?"

"Yes." Tom felt warm, and he brushed his thick brown hair back with one hand. His forehead was damp with sweat, despite the breeze blowing in through the curtains. "She's a journalism major, too. In fact, she had also applied for this internship. It was only luck that I got it."

"She had also applied . . ."

The intensity of Nicholas's stare seemed to sear across Tom's face before lighting on Elizabeth's photograph again. "Well, she's a very pretty young lady," Nicholas said easily. "Unusual looking."

"She's beautiful," Tom responded, not knowing why he was telling Nicholas this. It was too personal—none of Nicholas's business. But Tom couldn't help himself. "She's the most beautiful girl at Sweet Valley University. And her spirit . . . her spirit is beautiful, too." Tom blushed and looked down. Her *spirit?* Where had that come from? What was he talking about? He must have major jet lag.

"Yes," said Nicholas quietly. "I can see that. You're a very lucky young man." He took a deep breath, his chest rising and falling, though Tom heard no sound. "Now. I have some . . . commitments during the day tomorrow. Your assignment will be to go to the library at Tulane University and do some research. I have a list of questions written down, as well as some suggestions about possible sources. Tomorrow evening we can compare our notes."

Tom nodded. "Sounds good."

"I'll leave instructions with Fortune about when to pick you up, and Marielle will tend to your other . . . needs. And now I'll leave you to finish unpacking. I'm sure you must be exhausted."

Tom started to protest that it was still early, but when he glanced at the clock, he realized it was almost midnight. "Yes, I guess I am pretty tired. Thank you for everything, Nicholas. I'll see you tomorrow."

"Good night, Tom. I hope your stay here is pleasant."

After his host had left, Tom looked at the clock again in amazement, then checked his own watch. He couldn't believe how much time had passed. He would have sworn that he and Nicholas had sat talking together for no more than half an hour. Weird.

Tom walked back to his bedside table and picked up the wooden frame. Elizabeth looked off toward the horizon, wistful, distant. Tom traced the image of her cheekbone with one finger. Why had Nicholas been staring so intently at this picture?

Elizabeth, I miss you so much. I wish you were here. Feeling almost feverish, Tom put down the frame and went to stand in front of his open window. The long curtains brushed his body, winding around his legs. In the distance he could see the reflected lights of the rest of the French Quarter. He could hear the thin, tinny wisp of someone playing a saxophone far away.

I need some sleep.

Feeling a bit foolish, Tom closed and locked the windows. He crossed to the hall door and locked it also, then took the key and placed it on his bedside table. The ceiling fan overhead turned lazily, stirring up currents of moist air, ruffling his bedcovers. Elizabeth's picture caught his eye again. With a tiny frown he took the picture and put it back in his duffel bag.

Tom pulled back the covers and fell against the cool, welcoming sheets. It was only then that he remembered he had forgotten to call Elizabeth.

Bent over from the waist, Elizabeth pulled a brush through her long blond hair. It was late, but she had stayed up studying, afraid she wouldn't be able to get to sleep.

I'm glad this day is over, she thought. When I wake up tomorrow, it'll be less than forty-eight hours till Tom is back. The thought was comforting.

The golden strands of her hair swept the floor as

she methodically pulled the brush through, again and again. The rhythm was soothing. She was glad Jessica was out somewhere, and not there, talking, playing music too loudly, trying on different outfits.

Elizabeth smiled and sat up, throwing her hair over her back. She began brushing it again. Jessica was too much sometimes. Only time would tell what would happen with the Theta room. On one hand, Jessica usually got what she wanted. On the other hand, her complicated schemes had been known to backfire—especially when Alison Quinn was involved.

Again and again Elizabeth had become part of Jessica's plans against her better judgment; each time she had gone down in flames because of it.

But what I can do? She's my only twin.

Putting down the brush, Elizabeth changed into her long flannel nightshirt. Then she walked to her desk and picked up her favorite picture of Tom. The photograph showed him lying against the pillows on her bed, smiling up at the camera. His thick hair was messy, and his shirt was twisted around a little bit, showing an inch of skin above his black jeans. Elizabeth remembered snapping the picture—they had been taking a short break from studying, and suddenly she had jumped up and grabbed her camera. While Tom laughed up at her, she stood over him on her bed and aimed the lens down. She loved the open expression she'd captured on film. His dark eyes were shining and mischievous, and he looked relaxed and happy. His mouth was parted in a grin.

Oh, Tom, I love you so much. Glad that Jessica wasn't around to see her acting so sappy, Elizabeth bent and kissed his picture. Then she put it back on her desk, feeling better. All day she had felt strange and off balance, as if waiting for something awful to happen. And she had been upset earlier when Tom hadn't called to say he had arrived safely. In the end she had called the New Orleans airport herself. It had been a huge relief to find that his plane had landed with no problems.

"He's probably just really busy," she told herself. "He'll call tomorrow."

Crash! Elizabeth jerked around, startled. Out of nowhere, rain was lashing against her dorm window, and the sky was lit by a jagged bolt of lightning. The boom of thunder followed almost immediately.

Quickly, Elizabeth went to shut the window. Rain was already stinging against the glass, hitting it with force. *Weird. No storm was predicted for today. I hope Jessica's not caught in it.* For another minute Elizabeth watched the play of lightning on the quad. Then, feeling vaguely uneasy all over again, she lowered the shade, got into bed, and turned off the light. It was a long time before she fell asleep.

Chapter Five

"OK, that's eleven feet, eight inches," Jessica muttered, taking her pencil out of her mouth so she could write down the figure. The metal tape measure sucked itself back into its casing as Jessica paced off the room in the other direction.

Fresh morning sunlight poured through the bare windows, and Jessica opened one, inhaling the clean, rain-washed scent of a beautiful autumn day.

"And that looks like about thirteen feet." Jessica sketched a quick outline of the room's dimensions in her notebook. It wasn't often that she was up at the crack of ten on a Saturday morning. But she had been determined to attack the room problem ruthlessly. Sometimes that was the only way to succeed.

Already this morning she had subtly worked at getting some fellow Thetas on her side. She had spoken with Magda, Alexandra Rollins, and Denise Waters—not even mentioning the room. Instead she had just been pleasant and friendly, chatting about Theta concerns, the Monster Madness party, and other light topics. The point was to leave them with a positive, nonpushy, nongrasping image of her. The more goodwill she spread around, the better. She hoped that when push came to shove, people would be on her side.

Standing at one end of the room, Jessica mentally began placing furniture. She would have to buy a few new things; that was obvious. She couldn't use any dorm furniture, not that she'd want to. And when she had lived with Mike, he'd already had his own furniture. This room would be Jessica's first chance to really express herself by her surroundings, her first adult decorating attempt. And she knew just what approach she wanted to take—something wild, but not tacky. Eclectic, but not hodgepodge. When she finished with this room, people would be suitably impressed by her superior sense of style.

"What do you think you're doing?" The voice behind her dripped acid.

Jessica didn't even bother turning around. *I'll put a sofa over there,* she thought. "What do you want, Alison?" she asked in a bored tone.

"I'd like you to get out of my room," Alison replied.

Sparing Alison an indifferent glance, Jessica paced off the room in the other direction, then examined the windows. Curtains? Balloon shades?

"Did you hear me?" Alison's voice was quivering with barely suppressed anger.

"Uh-huh," Jessica drawled, measuring the width of one window. "So?"

"So I want you out of this room."

Finally Jessica turned and faced her archenemy. "The only prob, Alison, is that this isn't your room," Jessica explained painstakingly. "Your room is upstairs. We all know that. This happens to be my room. The sooner you wrap your mind around that concept, the better off we'll all be."

"You haven't won yet, Jessica Wakefield," Alison hissed. "This is going to be my room. You're going to stay over in Dickenson Hall with your drippy twin, where you belong. And the sooner *you* wrap *your* tiny mind around that concept, the longer you'll live." With a final sneer twisting her face, Alison stalked out of the room.

"Excuse me. Could you tell me where to find the Louisiana Collection?" Tom stood in front of the information desk at the Tulane University library on Saturday morning. After a solitary breakfast served by a hovering Marielle, Tom had dismissed Fortune's offer of a ride uptown. Instead he had walked through the French Quarter to

Canal Street, where he caught the streetcar.

The Quarter was amazing, he'd decided. Some of the buildings dated back to the 1700's and everywhere there was a strong influence of Spanish architecture and style, and French language and customs. The streets were narrow and clogged with slow-moving traffic, and even at an early hour there were street musicians and hawkers in front of T-shirt shops. Eager tourists, some of them wearing name tags proclaiming they were members of the United Dentists of America Association, milled through the streets, looking into the windows of the expensive antique stores lining Royal Street.

Tom had crossed Canal Street, a wide, six-lane boulevard. Marielle had told him where to catch the streetcar, and what stop was closest to Tulane University. Tom had hung out of the open window of the trolley and snapped pictures to take home to show Elizabeth. The streetcar went up the median of St. Charles Avenue—one of the main streets uptown, according to the tourist map he had bought. The avenue was wide, but with only one lane of traffic in each direction. There was surprisingly little traffic, compared to Los Angeles or even parts of downtown Sweet Valley. Huge oak trees with trunks three or four feet in diameter spread gnarled branches over the street, meeting in the middle to form a tunnel of green.

And now he was at the Tulane library. Even more than the night before, he felt as if he were a million miles away from California, from Sweet Valley, from Elizabeth. *Relax. This is the opportunity of a lifetime,* he told himself.

He looked down at the book the librarian had recommended. *Religious Holidays in Louisiana.* He had never thought of Halloween as being religious—basically, it was a time to get dressed up, pretend to spook yourself, and eat enough candy to rot your teeth for the rest of the year. But people here, especially those who still practiced some form of voodoo, regarded Halloween in a very different light.

Tom shook his head. Usually he loved being in new places—he dreamed of life after graduation, when he would travel on assignment all over the world. And he loved learning about new things, new cultures, new customs. Intense curiosity about anything and everything was the hallmark of a good reporter. So why was he homesick after only one day? Why was he uncomfortable in a beautiful, fascinating, historic city like New Orleans? Why had he locked his doors last night?

It was hot in the library. Tom undid the top two buttons of his shirt and ran his finger around his collar. The prick of sweat irritated the back of his neck, and Tom squirmed in his seat. He looked out the window to where the sun was shining through the oak trees. Big, puffy white clouds were lumbering across a deep-blue sky. He forced himself to turn back to his book. He had a job to do.

Elizabeth lifted her hair and quickly pulled it to the side so she could trap it in a fast braid. Then, sighing, she turned the page of her American-poetry textbook. Around her the SVU library was an empty, cavernous shell. *Of course,* she thought wryly. *It's a beautiful Saturday afternoon. Why would anyone be in the library?*

It had been hard to walk across the green quad on the way to the library. The sun was shining, the air was a tiny bit crisp, leaves crunched underfoot. People had been lying on the grass in the sun, reading or talking. Others were playing football. A black dog with a bandanna tied around its neck was making spectacular leaps, catching a Frisbee in its mouth, then proudly prancing back to its owner to drop the thing at his feet.

And Elizabeth had walked by them. Tonight she had plans to meet her best friend, Nina Harper, for dinner and a movie, but right now she had to get some studying done. Jessica had been in their room, making phone calls in an attempt to garner support in her Get-the-Room campaign. Distracted by the noise, Elizabeth had packed up and headed to the library.

Now she was sitting at a carrel, and the library was so silent and dead inside that she could hear the tiniest cough or scrape of a chair from far away.

OK, American poetry. Once again she turned her attention to her book, rereading a famous Randall Jarrell poem. She was dimly aware of quiet footsteps headed her way but refused to acknowledge them. Next week there was an essay test, and she had to be prepared.

"Elizabeth—I thought that was you."

The soft voice behind her made her jump. She laughed awkwardly as she recognized Ben Alsup, from her American-poetry class. Ben had sat behind her for most of the year, and he seemed like a nice guy.

Smiling, she flipped her book so he could see what she was reading. He smiled and sat down in the carrel next to her.

"Getting ready for next week's test?" he asked in a low voice.

Elizabeth nodded. "A couple of these poems are hard to analyze—some of the later ones."

"I know what you mean," Ben said. His curly auburn hair caught the fluorescent light from above, and his blue eyes smiled into hers. "I have to admit I get kind of lost when things quit rhyming."

"I like old-fashioned poems better, too," Elizabeth agreed. She had never really talked that much with Ben before, but now she realized that

60

her impression had been correct—he was a great guy. As they sat and compared notes about various poems they thought might be on the test, Elizabeth felt her day brightening. *And tomorrow Tom will be home.*

"Elizabeth," Ben said, a trace of self-consciousness coming over him. "I was wondering . . . if you aren't doing anything tomorrow, do you think, well . . . do you think maybe you'd want to go out with me? There's a seafood place not far up the coast—they have the best shrimp around."

For a moment Elizabeth's startled eyes met his blue ones. *He's asking me out on a date. Isn't he? Yes. He is.* "Oh, Ben," she said, a smile creating the dimple in her left cheek. "That's really sweet of you. It sounds great, but—you know I'm seeing Tom Watts, right?"

Ben shrugged, looking good-naturedly abashed. "I just thought, you know, you might be ready for a change or something."

Laughing, Elizabeth said, "No, Tom and I are still going strong. But if that ever changes, you'll be the first to know. OK?"

"Yeah, OK," Ben said, taking his rejection easily. "Just thought I'd ask."

"Well, thanks, I appreciate it," Elizabeth said. "You've made my day."

"Anytime. Well, take it easy—I'll let you get back to postwar poetry." With a final, friendly smile, Ben gathered his books and sauntered toward another reading room.

What a sweetie, Elizabeth thought, watching him walk away. If she weren't dating Tom, Ben was just the kind of guy she'd hope would ask her out. But she *was* with Tom, very much so. In the past they'd had their ups and downs—but lately they had never been closer or more in love. There was no way Elizabeth would jeopardize their relationship by getting close to another guy.

In a way her feelings for Tom were almost scary, she thought ruefully. It was as if she actually needed him in a physical, chemical way. He was only her second serious boyfriend—she'd dated Todd Wilkins all through high school. But even though she'd assumed she and Todd would always be together, somehow she'd never felt for Todd what she felt for Tom. When she'd been separated from Todd, she hadn't experienced this overwhelming sense of loss.

Sighing, Elizabeth repeated her mantra: *One more day.* Then she tossed her braid over her shoulder, leaned her chin on her hand, and applied herself to her book.

Chapter Six

"*Myths and Legends of Louisiana, The Unique History of Vlad the Impaler, Architecture of the Old South, The Causes of War in Modern Bosnia, Vampire Legends of the World* . . ." Tom read the book titles under his breath as he scanned the shelves in Nicholas's library. This had to be the weirdest collection of books he had ever seen in someone's home.

The library was a huge room on the first floor of Nicholas's house, with tall French windows looking out onto the backyard. Earlier, when Tom had just returned from the Tulane library, he had explored the rear garden. As in the front of the house, everything was wildly overgrown. There were several huge oak trees dripping with gray, lacy Spanish moss. A crumbling fountain stood in the middle of the yard, trickling green water from a statue of a young girl into a scummy pond below. In the garden Tom could no longer hear the sounds of the city that stood just outside the high brick walls. He could hear only the quiet trickle of the fountain, the rustling of dried leaves on the ground, the whisper of the wind passing through the thick growth of trees and plants.

In some ways New Orleans reminded Tom a little of California. Mostly in the weather, which was unseasonably warm, as it was back home. The air was wetter here, but it didn't have the smog so prevalent in southern California. Just like California, there weren't a lot of color-changing trees: maples, sycamores, birches. The live oaks stayed green year-round, and there were plenty of palm trees, banana plants, and sweet olives that seemed indifferent to the change of seasons.

But sitting inside, the sun having gone down, Tom felt that no place could be more different from his home than New Orleans. Everything in California seemed new, large, clean, and bright. Although equally beautiful, New Orleans was just the opposite.

Nicholas's library fit in perfectly with New Orleans' atmosphere, Tom thought. There was a small fire in the fireplace, though it was still in the sixties outside. The warm flames dispelled damp more than actual chill. The library walls were covered floor to ceiling with dark bookcases filled with thousands of volumes. Heavy, dark wood furniture, ornately carved and covered with deep-red leather, stood about in cozy groupings. The curtains were heavy tapestry and looked very old. In places they were almost rotten, Tom noticed, and they were dull with dust.

But the books were the oddest thing. Some of them were hundreds of years old—they must have been worth a fortune. Their leather spines, inlaid with gold, were stiff and cracked, their pages yellow and brittle. There were modern books as well; perhaps Nicholas used them in his job. They were about politics, world geography, world cultures, myths and legends and folklore, books on religion and philosophy.

"I'll have to ask him about some of these," Tom said aloud, tracing his finger along some of their spines. "But I better have something ready to show him when he gets back tonight."

Tom had found a lot of useful material at Tulane that day, and now he was settled at the library's massive desk, trying to organize his notes on his computer. He wasn't sure when his host would be back—it was almost seven thirty. Tom's stomach was already rumbling for dinner.

Bent over his computer, he tried to concentrate on his research, but soon he became aware of a tingling sensation in the back of his neck. He turned around, but there was nothing there. The shadows thrown by the fire were long and spiky, and Tom got up to snap on several more lamps around the room. That was better. He took his seat again. A few minutes later he moved his chair so that it was turned a little more toward the door. Now no one could come in without his noticing. *Why did I do that?* He shrugged, not wanting to examine his reasons too closely.

In the very next second he whirled around, unable to take the being-watched sensation any longer. Marielle, the housekeeper, was standing in the doorway, watching Tom with a tiny smile curling the edges of her lips.

Tom was so surprised by her presence that he couldn't think of anything to say. Instead he stared at her, absorbing her presence. She was perhaps twenty-one or twenty-two. Her hair was very dark, and cut in feathery layers that floated around her hair like wisps of down. Large coffee-brown eyes were set off by her smooth, tan skin. Next to her Tom felt like a hulking gargantuan—her frame was slight, and she was several inches shorter than Elizabeth. As usual, she was wearing a plain black dress and a white apron, her old-fashioned and matronly outfit making her exotic face and womanly body that much more incongruous.

Marielle raised her eyebrows at him but said nothing. In confusion Tom swallowed hard, feeling that the room had suddenly become stiflingly hot and close.

Small feet encased in dark stockings and shoes padded silently over the ancient Persian carpet toward him. Feeling like a dragonfly held by one wing, Tom could only watch her approach. Her eyes were so warm, so big, so welcoming. A man could drown in her eyes. Her mouth was so full. . . .

"Ah, Tom. It's good to see you being so industrious."

Nicholas's smooth, precise voice floated over to Tom and woke him like a dash of cold water.

"Nicholas," he said, getting to his feet. "I'm glad you're back." *Really glad. Gladder than you'll ever know.* "I've got some interesting stuff to show you—the Tulane library was really helpful. I've just been sitting here going over my notes."

"Fine, fine," Nicholas said with a smile. "But first, let's have dinner, shall we? Marielle? I believe you're needed in the kitchen."

Cool green eyes seemed to send Marielle a hidden message that Tom could only begin to pick up on. But he felt relief when the housekeeper demurely left the library and disappeared down the hall.

"Come," said Nicholas, giving Tom a reassuring smile. "Let's sample the local cuisine."

"So are you coming?" Jessica outlined her lips with fresh gloss. She checked herself in the mirror, then took off her headband and refluffed her hair.

"Nah," Elizabeth said, lying on her bed. "I'm supposed to see Nina in a little while. I'm meeting her at the cafeteria at seven." She raised one leg and examined a tiny bleach spot on her jeans. Should she change? No. Not for an evening with Nina.

"Oh, now *that* sounds exciting," Jessica said, turning one way and then another to look at her outfit from all angles. "Why don't you bail on Nina and come with us instead? Isabella, Lila, and I are checking out that new place on the beach—the one where all the waiters are struggling models and actors."

Elizabeth smiled. "Gee, maybe I should. Maybe I really *need* to go to some club, toss down a couple of diet Cokes, and then flirt outrageously with some good-looking airhead."

Jessica turned and grinned. "Works for me," she said cheerfully.

Laughing, Elizabeth tossed a sneaker at her twin. Jessica shrieked in mock outrage and furiously brushed off her black legging.

"Seriously, are you sure you don't want to come?" Jessica asked.

"No, thanks," Elizabeth replied, rolling off her bed and checking her watch. "Dinner and a movie with Nina are fine with me."

"Pardon me while I yawn," said Jessica. "Just don't say I didn't ask you. And don't wait up." She quickly stuffed her keys, wallet, and makeup bag into a black leather purse. "OK, gotta run."

"Have a good time," Elizabeth said, starting to put on her shoes.

"You know it. Oh, and if you wake up in the middle of the night and hear weird noises, don't turn on the light."

"Jessica!" Elizabeth cried, her eyes wide.

Laughing, her sister pulled the door closed, and Elizabeth heard her high-heeled boots clicking down the hall.

"It would be just like her, too," Elizabeth muttered, redoing her hair in its barrette. "That's the scary thing." After checking her face and deciding that it wasn't worth doing anything to, Elizabeth glanced at her watch. She had a few minutes to kill. An idea that had been perking in the back of her mind all day suddenly popped up again.

Call Tom. It was almost nine o'clock in New Orleans. Maybe he had tried to call that afternoon when Jessica had been hogging the phone for hours. And tonight she was going out—she might miss his call later. She felt as though they had been separated for months instead of barely more than twenty-four hours. He must be working really hard, she thought. Maybe he just couldn't get to a phone. Who knew what Nicholas des Perdu was making him do?

That decided it. She would call him. The address and phone number of where he would be staying, at Nicholas's house, had been on Tom's acceptance letter. Tom had given her a copy before he'd left.

Is it stupid to call him? Will it make him look unprofessional?

I don't care.

Before she could change her mind, Elizabeth pulled out her copy of the letter. Then, taking a deep breath, she dialed the phone number. In her mind she rehearsed what she would say. *Hello, may I please speak to Tom Watts? Hello, is Tom Watts there, please?* On the other end the phone rang several times. No one answered. Then an obnoxious whining tone sounded loudly in Elizabeth's ear, and she grimaced.

"I'm sorry. The number you dialed has been disconnected," said the automaton voice of the operator. "Please check your number and dial again."

Elizabeth did, but the result was the same. ". . . has been disconnected," Elizabeth mimicked the operator in frustration. After a moment's thought she dialed directory assistance in New Orleans.

"Could you give me the number for Nicholas des Perdu, please?" Elizabeth asked the operator. "On Chartres Street?"

There was a pause as the operator punched the information into her computer. "I'm sorry," she came back after a second. "That's an unlisted number."

"Unlisted?" Elizabeth was nonplussed. Then she remembered that Nicholas was something of a celebrity. He probably had crackpots calling him all the time. Of course he had an unlisted number. "Oh, I see," Elizabeth said. "Well, I have a number here that he gave me—I'm doing some work for him. If I read it to you, could you just tell me if it's correct? It's very important that I get in touch with him."

"I'm sorry," the operator said. "We're not allowed to do that. All I can say is that it's unlisted."

"Please?"

"I'm sorry," the operator said, and hung up.

Elizabeth stared at her phone, wanting to throw it against the wall. Unlisted! Disconnected! She was a thousand miles away from Tom, and she had no way to contact him, no way to get in touch. Was that why he hadn't called?

Don't they have pay phones in New Orleans?

"Wonderful!" Elizabeth banged the phone down and looked at her watch. Now she was a few minutes late. Great. Grabbing her jean jacket, Elizabeth flew out of her room and slammed the door. She needed some sympathy, fast.

I definitely have to call Elizabeth tonight, Tom thought. He hadn't called her yesterday, and he knew she'd be both worried and irritated. If he'd been thinking straight, he would have called her

71

from the library today. But for some reason, ever since he'd arrived in New Orleans, his mind hadn't been that clear. He'd had more spurts of wild imagination and capricious thinking than he'd ever had in his life.

But now it was about ten o'clock back in Sweet Valley. Even though it was Saturday night, there was a chance Elizabeth would be home.

Stifling a yawn, Tom emptied his pants pockets onto the dresser in his room. Then he looked around for a phone. Nope. No phone. There had been one in the hall, he remembered. He would use his calling card, so Nicholas shouldn't mind.

The wide hall outside his room was lined with huge, dark armoires and ornately carved chests with marble tops. On the wall were almost life-size portraits of aristocratic-looking men. Tom decided that if this was his house, the portraits would have to go. It was just too creepy to walk down the hall with all those eyes on him.

The phone was practically an antique; it was massive, black, heavy, and had a rotary dial. So much for his calling card. Well, he would tell Nicholas about the call tomorrow and offer to pay for it. Tom picked up the clunky receiver and started to dial Elizabeth's number.

He had barely got through the area code when he frowned and rubbed his hand across his eyes. Jeez, he was exhausted. He could hardly keep his eyes open. Now, where was he? One, two, one, three . . . was he up to the five yet? Tom blinked heavily and shook his head. Feeling as if a fog were overtaking him, he raised his head and found himself looking into the bottomless brown eyes of Marielle. She smiled up at him, and it was like the sun coming from behind a cloud to warm his skin.

Moving silently, she walked over to the open door of his room, then turned and looked back at him. Her eyes were smoky, luminous in the hallway's dim light. Her black hair floated around her face like a cloud. Without even thinking about it, Tom clumsily hung up the phone and walked toward her.

Chapter Seven

Tom followed Marielle into his room and over to his huge four-poster bed. The gauzy mosquito netting was looped back by the headboard, the heavy curtains pushed aside. Marielle leaned against the high mattress, still smiling her enigmatic smile. A cool breeze was swirling in through the open windows, and Tom became almost overwhelmed by a hauntingly sweet scent. Was it Marielle? Was it coming from outside? It didn't matter.

Slowly Tom approached the small black-garbed figure. He had never seen such an enticing woman in his life. He felt almost light-headed, incapable of speech. His movements felt clumsy and slow. Still, he reached out for her, felt the warmth of her shoulders through her dress. Her skin, up close, was smooth and rich and warm. She looked delicious.

Come to me. Her thought entered his head like

a memory. He was losing himself in her eyes. Then she blinked and turned her head for a moment, looking toward the desk lamp with a steady gaze. The lamp flickered and went out, leaving them in darkness save for the moonlight slanting in through the tall open windows.

The darkness made it easy for Tom to let go. His heart pounding, a faint sheen of sweat filming his forehead, he leaned closer, pressing his body against hers. She wrapped her arms around his back. Feeling as though he were watching himself in some silent, slow-motion movie, Tom lowered his head and gently kissed Marielle's neck. She held him close, and he could feel her cool breath against his cheek. Then she pulled away long enough to look into his eyes. She took his head between her small, strong hands and brought his face down for a deep, slow kiss.

Colors burst behind his eyes as he gave himself up to the sensation. It was as though he had never been kissed before, never felt this intense, white-hot rush of pleasure and desire.

He felt drugged now, ecstatic with the sensations he was feeling. He didn't care what Marielle did, as long as she didn't stop. Soon she was kissing his face, smoothing his hair back with her cool hands, running her palms along his chest and back. His breath came in fast, heavy rasps. Gently Marielle nibbled at his neck, kissing him. When she gently bit his neck, he laughed.

Tom's eyes were closed; he could feel his heart beating with a thick, fast-paced thud. There was only Marielle, the softness of her skin, her white teeth in the moonlight. . . .

Tom opened his eyes. For a split second he thought a strand of sun-streaked blond hair was trailing against his chest. *Elizabeth*, he thought dreamily, a smile crossing his lips. *Kiss me.* Then the woman kissing him raised her head. He realized that instead of looking at Elizabeth's beautiful, sun-fresh face, he was facing Marielle's dusky beauty, her knowing eyes.

Tom frowned, his hands freezing on Marielle's arms. It was like waking up. Quickly, his hands ineffectually pushed Marielle away.

"No, *cher*," she murmured. "Hold me." She pulled him a little closer and pressed her lips to his neck. Again he felt the pressure of her shiny teeth. With a force that surprised him, he jerked himself out of her arms.

He raked his hair back with one hand, not looking at her. Without saying anything he strode to the open windows and quickly gulped in some brisk night air. Dark, wispy clouds floated across the yellow moon. After a few moments Tom felt the first whisper-soft streaks of rain hitting his face. He closed his eyes and held his face up, letting the rain wash over him, letting it cool his skin. He didn't know how long he stood there—perhaps only minutes, perhaps hours. When he turned around, Marielle was gone.

What's wrong with me? Tom felt unclean, exhausted, and confused. He couldn't wait to get back home. There were just too many weird things about New Orleans—if he stayed there any longer, he would be ruined. The only thing he wanted now was to step off a plane in Sweet Valley and see Elizabeth's smiling face. *Elizabeth.* His betrayal of her almost choked him. Instantly he knew that he would never mention to her what had happened, that he would spend the rest of his life trying to make it up to her. He had been weak.

When he snapped on his bedside lamp, it threw shadows around the room. In the mirror over his dresser he saw that his eyes were dark and guilty. His mouth was swollen, as if he had been hit. There was a faint pink smudge on his neck where he could see small, indented teeth marks. Frowning, he examined them closer. She hadn't broken his skin, but the area ached, like a slight burn.

Elizabeth. After carefully locking his door and pocketing the key, he opened his duffel bag to get Elizabeth's picture. He needed to see her, see her sane eyes, her familiar face.

It was missing. Her picture was gone. Tom took everything out of the duffel, dumping it onto his bed, then went through his things one by one, shaking them out. His hands feverishly swept across the top of his desk, his chest of drawers. He searched the carpet, beneath the bed, among the clothes in the dresser—but her picture was definitely missing. A feeling of intense weariness and hopelessness came over him. *It must be here. It must be here.* Tomorrow it would turn up.

Suddenly Tom was so tired that he could think of nothing but going to sleep. He pulled the windows shut and locked them. Then he threw himself across the bed, closing his eyes to the world.

The candlelight flickered across Nicholas's face. *Lisette.* Delicately, he traced one slender finger down the smooth wood of the picture frame. The girl in the black-and-white photo gazed dreamily off into the distance. *Lisette.* Holding the frame to his chest, Nicholas moved in slow circles around his dark front parlor. A surge of joy, so long unfelt, so unfamiliar, was rising painfully in his chest. She had come back to him. He knew that she would. Something so beautiful, so rare, so precious, could never have been so impermanent.

"But why do you have to go, Nicholas?" Lisette's beautiful, troubled eyes looked at him reproachfully. "We're practically still on our wedding trip. Must you leave me?"

At his bride's imploring tone, Nicholas felt his throat close with pain. It would be so easy to stay by her side, so easy to pretend he had no other duties except to make her every waking moment a delight.

Crossing the salon, he took her small hands in his. "Darling, believe me," he said, his voice rough. "As a nobleman, I'm obliged to join Monsieur Lafayette in putting down the peasant uprising. It's the only thing a man of honor can do. But he assures me that it should take no time at all. And then you and I will be together again."

Her cool hand stroked his brow. He caught it and kissed the palm.

"How long will you be away?" she asked.

He looked at her, at her perfect beauty: the blue-green eyes, the golden hair, the delicate bones. To be away from her for even an hour was torture. But if he ignored his duty, he would never be welcome in his social circles again. He wouldn't be able to live with himself.

"No longer than I have to," he promised. "Perhaps only a few days. It's barely June, and I'm sure I'll be home before July. Surely the fighting won't last long—these people are armed with pitchforks and scythes. We'll have our swords and our muskets."

Lisette shuddered. "It's just—" Her voice broke. "It's just that I couldn't bear it if anything happened to you. I simply couldn't bear it."

Nicholas kissed her hand again. "Nothing will happen to me, I swear it," he said. "And while I'm away, I'll arrange for both of us to leave here afterward. Perhaps we can go to Germany or the Balkans for the rest of the summer. And then we won't have to think about this revolt."

Almond-shaped eyes beseeched him. "Really? We can go away?"

He smiled down at her. "Yes. It will be a continuation of our wedding trip."

Lisette smiled back at him, and he held her tightly against him. For long moments they stayed within the circle of each other's arms, their world complete. Nicholas could feel Lisette's heart, small and fierce, beating against his. Was such a love possible? Was such heaven truly available on earth?

"Listen," he murmured against silken hair, "while I'm gone, you must go nowhere. You may receive friends here, but I forbid you to open the doors to anyone you don't know and trust explicitly. Jacques and Fantime are staying here—you'll be safe with them. But you mustn't go anywhere outside—it's too dangerous. Do you understand? Do you promise me?"

"I understand," Lisette said soberly. "I promise."

"Good." He kissed her again. "Then I will go with a lighter heart, all the sooner to come back to you."

He bent to kiss her mouth, and they clung to each other as if their lives depended upon it.

In her dream Elizabeth was sitting at her desk, studying. The desk was anchored in a pool of yellow light in the middle of an enormous room, which was empty of furniture, of light, of life. Then a tall window blew open, and rain lashed against the grimy panes of glass. Rotted curtains, once beautiful, whipped inward like the sails on a ship. Red and yellow leaves, wet and decaying and smelling like autumn, blew into the room and swirled around her feet.

A faint sound made her turn. A tall figure dressed in black stood in the open window. Raindrops glistened against his night-dark hair. Bright bottle-green eyes seemed to pin Elizabeth to her chair. She felt no fear. *At last,* she thought.

Then she was standing in the middle of the room, and the lightning was casting huge, otherworldly shadows onto the chipped plaster of the faded walls. The figure came toward her, and now she could see his pale face; it looked as if it had been carved out of moonlight.

A strong, long-fingered hand reached out to her, and she felt a frisson of fear, as if a corpse in a grave had suddenly tried to pull her in. Eyes wide, heart pounding, she backed away, out of the circle of light into the darkness. Still the figure approached. The long pale hand reached for her again, and insidious tendrils of thought filtered into her brain. *Come to me, my beloved,* it said. *Come to me for all time.*

"No," she murmured, feeling as if she were choking. "No."

Her back hit something solid, something warm and firm, and she wheeled with a gasp.

"Oh, Tom!" she cried with relief, sagging against the familiar body, the hard chest, the comforting arms. "Tom, save me."

But when she looked pleadingly up at his face, a feeling of icy coldness came over her. It was Tom, but not Tom. His dark eyes stared straight ahead, through her and past her. His arms hung limp at his sides. Slowly he moved away from her. As Elizabeth watched in horror, Tom moved toward the tall, dark figure. One warm tan hand reached out to touch the cold pale one.

"No!" Elizabeth screamed in her sleep. "Tom, no!"

"Darn," Jessica muttered quietly as she struggled to wrench her key from her dorm-room lock. The darkness and silence of the room within told her that Elizabeth was already asleep. And after eighteen years of experience she knew that Elizabeth would not be very agreeable about being woken up. Finally Jessica got her key out and shut the door softly.

The light from the hallway was blocked out, and she paused for a moment to get her bearings. If she were simply making her way to Elizabeth's bed, there would be no problem. There was always a nice clear path from the door to Elizabeth's bed. But to navigate from the door to *her* bed was a different matter entirely. Basically, it should never be attempted in the dark, and even during the day one needed to use extreme caution. Stray shoes, laundry, discarded outfits, magazines, textbooks, a spare hairbrush—any or all of these could be lying underfoot.

With a sigh Jessica dropped her purse where she stood. Then she kicked off her high-heeled boots and pushed them behind her. Keeping her feet flat on the carpet, she shuffled forward, feeling her way slowly and carefully toward her desk. Once there, she clicked on her desk lamp and threw her long silk scarf over it, muting the light. She nodded with a satisfied grin. It actually looked very pretty.

Then, working fast, she gathered Elizabeth's bathroom things, shrugged out of her clothes, and threw on her own bathrobe, which was conveniently draped on top of her dresser. A glance at Elizabeth confirmed that the light hadn't awoken her.

Then Jessica was struck by the expression on Elizabeth's face. She was flushed in her sleep, and frowning. Her jaw was tense and her eyebrows knotted. Her breathing came shallow and fast, and she'd kicked her covers onto the floor.

She must be having a nightmare, Jessica realized with surprise. Very quietly she moved across the room and put her hand on Elizabeth's shoulder. As soon as she touched her sister, Elizabeth's face slackened and her tension eased. In another minute her face was relaxed and she was sleeping normally.

Jessica shook her head. *She was probably picturing herself getting a B-minus on a history quiz,* Jessica thought wryly. Shrugging, she shuffled noiselessly out the door and down the hall to the bathroom.

"Five more hours, and I'll see Elizabeth," Tom sang under his breath on Sunday morning. He rolled up his dirty laundry and stuffed it into his duffel bag. In just another hour he would be at the airport, and then he would be on his way home and away from this place. Elizabeth would be waiting for him, and as soon as they hugged, everything would be all right. His passionate minutes with Marielle would be nothing more than a bad dream.

While he was throwing his notebooks into his bag, his fingers brushed something cool and smooth. He pulled it out. Elizabeth's picture.

84

Vaguely he remembered searching for it the night before and not being able to find it. The memory was hazy. Now it was obvious that it had been there all along. Smiling, Tom allowed himself a long, lingering glance at Elizabeth's face. *I tried to call her last night. Didn't I? I didn't talk to her.* Marielle had shown up then. But there had been something odd, even before Marielle had arrived. Something about the phone, something weird. What was it? His fingers brushed at a spot on the photograph. With a frown Tom examined it more closely. He could have sworn there was no spot before—what was it? Looking at the picture closely, he saw that the dot was a dark red blotch, tiny and almost unnoticeable. As if something had spilled on the glass of the frame and dried. He scratched at the stain with his fingernail, then shrugged when it didn't come off. With a last, longing gaze he packed the photograph into his duffel bag, sandwiching the treasure carefully among his clothes.

"Note to myself: Don't come back to New Orleans for a long time," Tom said aloud. He double-checked the desk and the chest of drawers, making sure he hadn't forgotten anything. It was about eleven o'clock in the morning, but so far his host hadn't put in an appearance. Tom had woken up with a clear head and filled with new resolve. He'd just experienced the weirdest two days of his life, but still, he felt that he had done a good job for Nicholas.

85

After their dinner the previous night, and before the horrible scene with Marielle, he and Nicholas had sat in the downstairs library for hours, going over Tom's notes and discussing the nature of Nicholas's planned article. Nicholas had seemed impressed with Tom's research, and pleased about some of the bizarre customs and rituals Tom had unearthed at the Tulane library.

"That's what's important," Tom told himself. "I did good work—that's all that matters. Nothing else that happened here counts. It's forgotten." Nodding his head decisively, Tom set his packed duffel bag by the door. He really should go find Nicholas and thank him for the internship.

The next moment it was as if the sun had been plucked from the sky. The bedroom was suddenly dark, the furniture shrouded in shadows. His brow creased in confusion, Tom went to the windows and looked out just as the first fat raindrops started splashing against the panes. The sky, which had been bright just a few minutes ago, was now the color of bruised eggplant. Malignant-looking clouds were closing in overhead, reaching thick fingers down to the tops of the buildings in the distance. A rolling chain of thunder rumbled so loudly that the glass rattled in the windows. Jagged splinters of lightning split the sky, again and again, always followed by booming thunder. Then rain fell—rain like none Tom had ever seen.

It looked as if someone were standing on the roof above him, dumping a barrelful of water over the edge, practically blocking Tom's view of anything but the balcony.

"Whoa," he muttered, gazing out at the rainstorm in front of him. It looked as if a hurricane had hit.

"Your flight has been delayed."

The husky voice, so close behind him, made Tom jump and almost hit his head on the window frame. Feeling a quick spurt of anger, he turned to see Marielle's inscrutable face. In the storm-darkened daylight she looked as beautiful as ever, but Tom hardened his heart and his mind against her.

"What do you mean, my flight is delayed?" he asked her harshly.

She gave an apologetic shrug. "The storm. Planes can't take off. I just heard it on the radio and called the airport. They think the storm will pass by sundown. You can leave then."

Tom stared at her. Delayed! He didn't care about the storm—he wanted to get back home *immediately*. The strangeness of the last two days, the embarrassing near seduction by Marielle, the fact that he hadn't spoken to Elizabeth since he'd left—all of these things suddenly rose in his mind and made him desperate to get out of New Orleans. The prospect of waiting even a few more hours made him want to break something.

"Are you sure?" he choked.

Marielle nodded. "I'm sorry," she said, not looking sorry at all. "Perhaps by sundown."

"Can I make a long-distance call?" Tom asked firmly. At least he could call Elizabeth and let her know he'd be late.

"I'm sorry," Marielle said again, seeming to take a peculiar pleasure in the words. "Right after I called the airport, the storm knocked out the phone. Perhaps later."

"Fine," Tom said abruptly, turning away from her. He took several deep breaths, trying to rein in his impatience. "Well, I'm all packed and ready to go. Please let me know when Fortune is ready to go to the airport."

Her voice, when she spoke, was even closer to him. He could almost feel her breath through the shirt on his back. "Yes, Tom, I will," she whispered. "I'll let you know when Fortune is ready."

Biting his lip, Tom wouldn't let himself turn around until he heard the quiet sound of the door closing behind her. Then he whirled, stalked to the bed, and punched the pillows as hard as he could. It was then that he realized what had been odd about the phone last night, when he had tried to call Elizabeth. There had been no dial tone.

Chapter
Eight

"Yeah," Elizabeth said on Sunday at lunch. She took a sip of orange juice. "The scarf caught on fire because Jessica left it on top of her lamp while she went to the bathroom."

"And the lamp was turned *on*?" Nina asked in disbelief. "As in, with a hot lightbulb?"

"That's right," Elizabeth said crisply. She took another bite of her vegetarian burrito. "The scarf caught on fire. Which of course made the smoke alarm in our room go off. Then I woke up to find the room full of smoke and Jessica's desk in *flames*—"

"Stop, stop," Denise Waters said from across the cafeteria table. "You're making this up. Jessica didn't really do that."

"Oh, no, she does things like this," Winston Egbert confirmed. "It comes naturally to her."

Winston had gone to the same grade school, middle school, and high school as Jessica and Elizabeth and had been hearing stories like the one Elizabeth was telling for years. Denise, his girlfriend, was one of Jessica's sorority sisters.

"Jessica was in the bathroom down the hall"—here Elizabeth couldn't stifle a giggle—"in her bathrobe, with *cold cream* all over her face—"

Denise and Winston started chuckling across the table.

"And she heard the main fire alarm for the dorm going off. And I was in the room with this fire—"

"What did you *do*?" Denise practically shrieked. "You could have been killed!"

"Everyone in the dorm could have been killed!" Winston pointed out.

"I put out the fire, of course," Elizabeth explained. "I smothered it."

"With what?" Nina asked. "Don't tell me you had a bucket of sand all ready, just in case."

Elizabeth dissolved into unstoppable giggles, and she had to give in to them for a couple of minutes. When she finally got a grip on herself, her face was pink.

"Nope. No sand. I used . . . something else. But it was a matter of life and death," Elizabeth defended herself. "Every second counted. I had to act on instinct."

"How did you smother the fire?" Winston pressed.

"With Jessica's leather jacket," Elizabeth confessed.

Denise's eyes widened. "Not her new one," she breathed. "Not the one she went without lunch for a month for."

"The room was on *fire*!" Elizabeth cried. "And the jacket was right there! Was I supposed to die to keep Jessica's coat from being ruined? I don't think so."

"Was it ruined?" Nina asked, pulling her soda closer and taking a sip.

Elizabeth nodded ruefully. "Yeah, it really was. And I guess I don't have to tell you that burning leather smells *awful*. Anyway, by then the firemen were trying to break down our door—" She tried hard not to start laughing again. "Our RA, Caryn, came with her passkey just as the firemen burst in and saw all the smoke in the room." Elizabeth shook her head, remembering the chaos. "And they smelled Jessica's burning coat, and they . . . and they thought it was *me*!" Elizabeth gasped.

"This is starting to sound like a bad episode of *Candid Camera*," Winston said.

Elizabeth nodded. "They actually thought I was on fire! Because of the smell of the burning leather! Naturally they all leaped into the room to save me, but Jessica had left a bunch of stuff right in front of the door, as usual. And the poor firemen tripped and fell smack on their faces on our floor—"

"What did Jess do?" Denise asked.

"She ran in wearing her bathrobe, with all this white gunk on her face. And she looked at the pile of firemen on our floor, and she looked at me with all the smoke, and she looked at the lamp where the fire was, and she said—"

"What? What?" Nina begged.

"She said, 'What have you done to my *jacket*?'" Elizabeth shrieked. Then she put her head down on her hands on the table and laughed, picturing Jessica's outraged face covered with cold cream, and the dumbfounded firemen.

For several moments everyone at the table howled with laughter.

"I never should have gone back to the library after we went out last night," Nina said, shaking her head. "The one time something interesting happens on our floor in Dickenson Hall, I miss it."

"I think you'll survive," Elizabeth said. "Besides, now you've got a week's worth of physics problems done."

"There's one thing I want to know," Winston said when he had more or less recovered. "What possessed Jessica to put a scarf on the lamp in the first place?"

"Oh," said Elizabeth, taking a few deep breaths. "Well, I was asleep, and she was trying not to wake me up."

Three pairs of eyes stared at her, and then they all broke out in laughter again.

When Elizabeth got back to her dorm room after lunch, Jessica was there, folding piles of laundry on top of her bare mattress.

Elizabeth looked around. There was still a faint smell of smoke in the room, but in general, things didn't look too bad.

"That cleaning service you hired this morning did a good job," she told her sister, noting how they had scrubbed every trace of soot off the furniture, ceiling, and walls.

"I still think you should chip in to help pay for some of it," Jessica said.

"Oh, yeah," Elizabeth said dryly, pulling the phone over to her desk. "Especially since it's all my fault. I mean, if I hadn't been sound asleep, minding my own business, none of this would have happened. I'm so inconsiderate sometimes."

Jessica pulled a pile of sheets and towels over and began folding them. "I was only thinking of you," she reminded Elizabeth in an injured tone. "You should be glad I woke you up. You were having a nightmare."

At the mention of her disturbing dream of the night before, Elizabeth felt a little shiver go down her spine. Then she shook her head, putting it out of mind. It had just been a dream.

"Uh-huh," Elizabeth said, flipping through the phone book. "Maybe next time a simple shake of the shoulder would do." She grinned at Jessica. "Don't feel you have to take extreme action on my account."

Jessica made a face at her.

Elizabeth cradled the phone against her neck. "What's the news on that room at Theta house? It's a done deal, isn't it?" She started to dial the number of Tom's airline.

"This *wasn't* my fault," Jessica insisted loudly. "But since you're so interested in getting rid of me, then yes, the room is definitely going to be mine. That should make you very happy."

Holding up one finger for silence, Elizabeth asked the airline's customer service about the status of Tom's flight. She checked her watch. It should be landing in about an hour, giving her plenty of time to get to the airport.

"I'm sorry," the ticket clerk told her. "Severe thunderstorms in the greater New Orleans area have delayed many of our flights. That flight is now scheduled to take off at six twenty-seven central standard time, arriving in Sweet Valley at seven nineteen Pacific time."

"What?" Elizabeth felt her heart constrict. She had been counting the seconds until she could head to the airport to pick up Tom. Now it looked as though she would have to wait five more hours. "I don't believe this."

"We're sorry, ma'am," the clerk said. "But New Orleans weather can be very unpredictable."

Elizabeth hung up the phone in frustration. "Tom's flight is late!" she cried. "He won't be in until tonight."

"Oh, that's too bad," Jessica said absently while she folded a cotton sweater. Then she looked up, her eyes bright. "So I can use the Jeep right now, since you won't need it."

"I guess so," Elizabeth sighed. "But try to be back by six, just in case his flight's early."

"No problem," Jessica promised, pushing aside the rest of the laundry. "I just wanted to get a few things for my new room."

"You know, we still have to go shopping for all the Monster Madness decorations," Elizabeth reminded her. "I have a list ready. I thought we could go to the Party Basket. When do you want to do it?"

"Um, today's Sunday," Jessica said, looking at the ceiling thoughtfully. "How about Wednesday? Or maybe Thursday?"

"OK," Elizabeth said. She flopped disconsolately on her bed. "But I don't want to leave it till the last minute. I guess we should decorate the old Hollow House on Friday during the day—neither of us have many classes. We also have to set up all the refreshments and the stuff for the band."

Jessica grabbed her purse and her keys. "Fine.

95

Just tell me when." Waving good-bye, she flew out the door.

On her own bare mattress, which still carried the faint, acrid smell of burned leather, Elizabeth sighed.

Outside his window, Tom saw that the rain had lessened from a raging storm to a steady, heavy downpour. He shivered and rubbed the towel over his head again. Unable to face the thought of another solitary meal served by a slinky Marielle, Tom had actually ventured out into the storm for lunch. It had been kind of exhilarating, actually. His trench coat firmly buttoned up to his collar, a newspaper over his head, he had run down the wet, leaf-covered brick path to the front gates of Nicholas's estate.

Outside, on the street, he'd been struck by the force of the rain and quickly darted beneath a nearby overhanging balcony. Once there he'd explored his options. It was Sunday, but everything had seemed to be open for business. Fortunately, there was an almost unbroken line of balconies covering the sidewalks, which had protected him from the worst of the rain. He would get wet, he'd reasoned, but maybe not completely and utterly soaked. Tom had set off toward Canal Street.

An hour later he'd leaned back in his chair at the Napoleon House on Chartres Street and patted his stomach. New Orleans was the weirdest, prettiest, creepiest town he had ever been to, but the food was fantastic. He'd had half a muffaletta sandwich and two bottles of Barq's root beer.

It had been a relief to be out of Nicholas's house. He hadn't noticed before how dark and oppressive the house seemed. Maybe it was because he'd been on his own so much there—he never saw Nicholas during the day. And he was now avoiding Marielle like the plague.

On his way back, Tom had bought a copy of that day's newspaper to replace the one that had got wet. He'd let himself back into the house and made his way to his room, seeing no one. Now he was drying off and wondering how to kill a few more hours. He sat down at the desk and picked up the newspaper.

"Another Woman Murdered" read a small headline on the front page. Tom frowned.

"A local woman was killed last night in what appears to be the city's latest crime spree," Tom read. "The body of Deborah Stoppard, twenty-nine, was found on the breakwater of the river between Dauphine and Conti streets in the French Quarter. Police estimate she had been dead only a few hours. No motive for the killing has been found, but as in two other recent murders, the cause of death was exsanguination."

Tom frowned. Exsanguination? Where had

he heard that word before? He read on.

"Exsanguination, or being bled to death, is one of the rarer murder methods," the article said, "since it takes a relatively long time. Police are keeping details confidential."

Tom quickly finished the article, but there was no other information. Being bled to death. *What a way to go*, he thought. That was another strike against New Orleans—too many weird murders. His watch showed that he should probably leave for the airport in about an hour; it was already almost five thirty and getting dark outside. The rain was now a misty drizzle.

Deciding to find Nicholas so he could thank him for his hospitality, Tom left his room. He made it downstairs without being waylaid by Marielle, but Nicholas was nowhere to be found. Neither was Marielle. The house seemed as silent and as empty as an abandoned theater.

Wandering through the rooms, Tom was again struck by how much they resembled a movie set. Everything was too perfectly period, too preserved. The house had no life in it, no sense of change.

Even the kitchen looked like a historic reproduction, Tom thought, carefully poking his head inside. There was no microwave, no modern stove. He didn't know how Marielle cooked in it, though the meals she had served had been very good. Across the kitchen was a tall unpainted door a few inches ajar. Did they have basements there?

After looking around cautiously, Tom made his way across the kitchen. He felt guilty snooping around someone else's house, but he told himself he was only trying to find Nicholas to thank him. The door opened silently when he pulled it, and he saw stairs leading downward into the darkness beyond. There didn't seem to be a light switch.

There was no reasonable excuse he could give for going into Nicholas's basement. Tom blamed it on irresistible reporter's curiosity. *Not to say nosiness,* he told himself. The stairs were rough, almost unfinished. The rickety banister felt splintery and none too safe under his hand. Still, Tom went down the first couple of stairs, allowing his pupils to dilate in the darkness.

Well, it's just a regular basement, he thought, beginning to make out the dim outlines of old furniture and household castoffs. He was aware of feeling a little disappointed. *What were you expecting?* he chided himself. *Dead bodies?* He peered down into the musty darkness. A rusted birdcage on a stand was near the bottom of the stairs; an old lamp, its shade now torn and hanging in forlorn shreds, stood next to it. Deeper in the shadows were large shapes less easy to make out. In the middle of the main area was a large boxlike—

"It's time for you to leave now."

Tom jumped and almost fell headfirst down the

stairs. When he regained his balance and turned around, he could see Marielle's small, dark figure outlined in the light from the kitchen. Her voice had sounded cold.

"Um," Tom stammered.

"Fortune is waiting to take you to the airport," the housekeeper said. She stood back in the doorway, and Tom reluctantly climbed the stairs toward her.

"Ah, do you know where Nicholas is?" Tom asked, aware that he was blushing with embarrassment, hating the fact that Marielle had found him in such a compromising position.

"He will come to say good-bye," Marielle said shortly, her brown eyes now looking as cool as smoky quartz. "Your bag is still upstairs."

"Um, OK," Tom said, feeling that Marielle definitely had the advantage.

Without looking back he left the kitchen and went up to his room to get his bag. Then he met the chauffeur by the front door.

"Mr. Watts," Fortune said, seeming to gaze deeply into Tom's eyes. Tom felt uncomfortable, unsure of what Fortune was looking for, or expecting to see.

"Hi, Fortune," Tom said. "I appreciate the ride to the airport."

"We deeply regret your leaving," came the precise, elegant tones of Tom's host.

Tom turned to see Nicholas, impeccably dressed as always, coming out of the library.

"Yes, well." Tom managed a smile. "I've really enjoyed being here," he lied. "And I really appreciate the internship. It was great working with you." This, at least, was true.

"You must come back to our beautiful city soon," Nicholas said, walking Tom out onto the wide front veranda overhung with thick, tangled wisteria vines, now bare for winter. It was dark outside, the autumn sun having sunk beyond the pink stucco buildings at the edge of the Quarter.

"Yeah, that would be great," Tom said. *Like maybe when I'm ninety years old.*

Nicholas smiled briefly, looking into Tom's eyes with amusement.

As if he could hear my thoughts, Tom observed uneasily.

"Oh, I was reading today's paper, and I saw an article that might interest you," Tom said, attempting to change the subject.

"Yes? What was that?" In the pale-yellow light of the porch lamp, Nicholas looked as refined and emotionless as porcelain. Out in the courtyard Fortune was pulling up in the long limousine.

"A series of deaths—women being bled to death," Tom said.

Bright-green eyes met his quickly, and Tom felt the swift breaking of sweat on the back of his neck.

"Why would that interest me?" Nicholas asked, still boring into Tom's eyes.

"Because . . ." Tom began, suddenly feeling as though he were being sucked beneath an overwhelming wave. "It's so close to Halloween. And the deaths are so weird. I was wondering if they had something to do with a voodoo cult . . . or something."

Fortune stepped out of the limousine and opened the back door for Tom. Smiling, Nicholas took Tom's bag and walked him out to the car.

"I doubt it," Nicholas said easily. "It's probably the work of some lunatic. Or, more likely, the police are just confused. You must forget about it."

"Um, yeah, OK," Tom said, suddenly wondering why he had even mentioned it. Nicholas was right—it was a stupid article. He didn't even know why the police had reported it. It meant nothing.

"Good-bye, Tom Watts," Nicholas said, helping Tom into the car. "I appreciate all your help. You've been most instrumental."

"I was glad to do it," Tom said. "And if you're ever in Sweet Valley, be sure to look me up."

"Oh, I will," Nicholas said silkily. "I will."

Then he slammed the door of the limo and walked back to the house. Through the smoked glass Tom could see Marielle waiting for

Nicholas at the door. He wondered if she had told Nicholas he had been snooping. He hoped not.

On the other hand, he'd never have to see either one of them again. And he was glad about it.

Chapter Nine

"Excuse me, sir. Please fasten your tray in its up-right and locked position." The flight attendant hovered over Tom until he did as she asked.

Gladly, Tom thought. *I'll do anything you want, since it means we're getting closer to home, and Elizabeth.*

Despite turbulence and lousy food, the flight had been one of the best of his life. The plane ride to New Orleans, only two days ago, seemed as if it had taken place in another lifetime.

Filing off the plane seemed to take forever, and Tom anxiously craned his neck to see over people's heads. There she was! Elizabeth's smiling face was stunningly beautiful.

In the next moment he had dumped his duffel at his feet and had swept Elizabeth up in a huge hug.

"Oh, Tom, I missed you so much," she murmured between kisses.

"I missed you, too," he breathed, feeling her arms around him, her soft hair brushing his cheek. Everything about her shouted comfort, safety, love. It was heaven.

"Is this everything?" Elizabeth asked, looking down at his bag.

"Yeah." Tom pulled her to him once again, and she giggled.

"Tom, everyone's looking," she whispered as he kissed her neck, her cheek.

"I don't care," he murmured, holding her tight. "I'm finally holding you again, and I'm never going to let you go."

Elizabeth pulled back and smiled up at him, her blue-green eyes alight with love. "That could make driving difficult."

Tom grinned back, his heart feeling light and happy and free, as though a dark burden had been lifted from him. "Not to mention bathing."

Laughing, they put their arms around each other's waists and headed for the airport exit.

The rain beat against the small airplane windows, and outside, flashes of lightning exploded around them. Several people on the plane murmured worriedly, peering out the clouded windows into the dark night beyond.

In his seat Nicholas allowed himself the brief fantasy of the plane's electrical systems going out, casting all the passengers in blackness. How much could he accomplish before the emergency backup came on? Who would he approach first? The fresh-faced young mother sitting across from him in first class? The strapping college athlete who had passed him on his way back to coach? A tingling, not unpleasant ache began in Nicholas's upper jaw, and he rubbed his hand across his mouth.

Lisette, I've been alone too long. I need your good-ness, your sweetness, to help me reform my ways. Soon we'll be together again—one love, inseparable by time or death. We will be immortal together, and it will be paradise on earth.

Another crack of thunder and flash of lightning made some of the passengers draw in their breath and whisper anxiously. Rain whipped against the thin aluminum body of the plane as the craft pitched and rolled in the thunderstorm. It was al-most like being on an old-fashioned wooden ship of two hundred years before, Nicholas thought. He enjoyed it. It brought back memories of the first time he had come to America. When was it? Eighteen-oh-something. It was hard to remember. Details, details . . .

"Ladies and gentlemen, we should be out of this storm soon," the flight attendant announced over the scratchy loudspeaker. "And our arrival in

Sweet Valley will be only a few minutes late." She went on with some information for those making connecting flights, but Nicholas tuned her out. He was making no connecting flight. Everything he needed was right there in Sweet Valley.

"These red-eye flights are murder, aren't they?" Nicholas's seatmate, a flushed-faced businessman who had been knocking back Scotches throughout the storm, shifted impatiently in his seat.

Nicholas inclined his head politely. "Like death," he agreed.

"OK, turn left up here." Elizabeth pointed to the turnoff Tom had to take to get to the old Hollow House. It was a beautiful Monday afternoon, Tom was right by her side, and Elizabeth felt happy and peaceful. It was as though a shadow had passed over her momentarily but now was gone.

"Wow, is that it?" Tom whistled as he pulled his Saturn wagon to a stop. "How come I've never been here before?"

"I don't know," Elizabeth said. A hint of a smile dimpled her left cheek. "I guess you just didn't feel like going to parties before you met me."

Tom nodded. "That must be it. But this place is awesome. Come on, let's go check it out."

It was broad daylight, and Elizabeth had Tom with her. Still, she felt the slightest tremor of trepidation as she fit the key into the lock on the massive front door. Memories of what had happened when she and Jessica had been there last week made her feel the tiniest bit apprehensive.

Quit being a sissy, she told herself. *You're eighteen, not six. Get a grip.*

"When Jess and I were here, we decided to put the bar and the food in the dining room, at opposite ends," Elizabeth said, leading Tom on a tour of the first floor. "And that will leave the big ballroom and the front parlor empty for the band and dancing."

"Yeah," Tom said, looking around thoughtfully. "Why don't you put another bar here, on the sunporch? That way there won't be just one big crush in the dining room."

"Oh, good idea," Elizabeth said, writing it down on her clipboard. "See, I knew it was smart to bring you here today."

"Where's Jessica, the Wonder Twin?" Tom asked, trying to look through a grime-encrusted window.

Elizabeth looked up with a wry expression. "I'm not sure, but I saw her piling the Jeep full of shopping bags. My guess is that she's at the Theta house, trying to stake her claim on that extra bedroom."

"Huh." Tom walked around the band's area at one end of the ballroom. "We'll need to build a little stage here," he said, motioning with his hands. "And maybe we should rent a portable generator, just in case the band's equipment overwhelms the wiring."

"Oh, great, great," Elizabeth said, writing down these suggestions as well. "I'm so glad I brought you here. I didn't even think of that stuff."

Tom shrugged, looking pleased and embarrassed at the same time. Elizabeth grinned at his modest expression.

"So," Tom said. "If Jessica moves to Theta house, would you get another roommate?"

Elizabeth groaned. The first time Jessica had moved out of their room, Elizabeth had been assigned the roommate from hell. Celine Boudreaux had not only smoked, drunk, and brought strange guys back to their dorm room, but in the end she had taken up with William White, the psycho who had tried to kill Elizabeth.

"That would be the last thing I need," Elizabeth said. "Maybe I could talk the RA into letting me have a single for a while."

Tom wiggled his eyebrows. "Good idea," he said brightly. "That sounds very . . . cozy. Cozy and private." His eager expression made Elizabeth roll her eyes.

"Don't be too obvious or anything," she said dryly. She clicked on the overhead light and started to count how many lightbulbs she would need to replace in the cobweb-strewn chandelier. The sun was just starting to go down, and the chandelier's weak yellow light didn't do much to dispel the gloomy atmosphere. "And don't get your hopes up. My having a single does *not* mean that you get to start staying over."

Tom put on a wounded expression. "I'm hurt," he said. "I'm really hurt that you would suspect me of ulterior motives. Of course, all I'm thinking is that you would be able to, uh, study more. Have peace and quiet to study in. That kind of thing."

"Uh-huh." Elizabeth brushed her hair out of her eyes. She began to make a list of what supplies the setup committee would need to bring on Friday morning. It was getting hard to see, and she checked her watch. "Wow, almost five thirty. What do you want to do for dinner?"

"How about the cafeteria? I have to go over some stuff at WSVU after dinner." Tom kicked at the worn carpet on the floor, raising a little cloud of dust.

"OK, fine with me. I've got a French test to study for. Now, I just need one more look at the dining room, to make a diagram for the refreshment tables, and then we can get out—"

Her words ended in a strangled yelp as the lights flickered, then went off.

"Oh, no, not again," she said. "Tom?"

"Right here, Liz," Tom said, his comforting voice coming closer. Seconds later he bumped into her. His strong arms circled her shoulders and helped dispel the rising fear that was coiling in her stomach. "Did this happen before?"

"Yeah, when Jessica and I were here. But we were alone, and it was about to storm, and we got scared and ran off." Elizabeth forced herself to laugh. "The next day I came back, and it was just a fuse. I got some extras, just in case, and left them by the fuse box in the basement."

"Look, you stay here—no point in both of us killing ourselves in the dark," Tom said, his voice even and confident. "I'll go change the fuse and be right back, OK?"

"That would be great," Elizabeth said, grateful for his offer. The basement had been really creepy during the day, and she had absolutely no desire to go down there at night. "I'll wait right here."

"OK." Tom kissed her on her head; then his arms left her, and she heard him start to make his way slowly out of the dining room. As soon as he was gone, the air seemed ten degrees colder, and she shivered. In the dark, empty room her ears strained for any sound. But all she heard was the trees brushing against the windows, the very faint, far-off sounds of cars on the road, and Tom's loud swearing when he knocked into something.

In the next moment strong arms enclosed her again, and Elizabeth almost screamed.

"I missed you so much," a voice whispered in her ear.

"Tom." Elizabeth sighed with relief and relaxed against him. "I thought you were going to see about the fuse."

"Shh."

Before Elizabeth could speak again, she felt a brush of cold air cross her face. Then firm, cool lips pressed against hers.

This is what I need, Elizabeth thought happily as she kissed him back. *Good old-fashioned romance. It makes the world go round.*

To Elizabeth's surprise the kiss deepened, the pressure increased, and her head began to swirl deliciously. She and Tom had been together for a while, and there had always been a lot of chemistry between them. For the most part, they both tried to be very careful about how far they let themselves go when they were together. Bitter experience had taught them that going a little too far and then having to stop was much more painful than never getting started in the first place.

But it seemed as if Tom had forgotten about that for now, Elizabeth thought giddily as wiry arms pulled her even closer against his body. *Sometimes he seems so tall,* she thought dreamily. *Taller and thinner than he looks.*

On and on they kissed, until Elizabeth felt that she was drowning in a wonderful maelstrom of desire and passion. *Wow*.

"Hmm, Tom," she murmured when she came up for a moment of air. "Tom, what's come over you? No—don't answer. Just kiss me again. I like it."

I more than like it, she admitted to herself. *I love it*.

A warm voice, or rather, more of a sensation than a voice, answered her within her own mind.

I love you. I've missed you so much. Ached to hold you for so long, beloved.

Smiling, Elizabeth wrapped her arms more tightly around him, pressing her body against his. Just a few minutes ago she was scared, cold, and alone in this abandoned, run-down mansion. Now it seemed like the most wonderful, romantic place in the world. It was like a fantasy, like a romantic dream that had come true.

And then, just as suddenly as it had begun, the kiss was over. Iron-hard arms left her body, the cool mouth that had become hot and smoldering against hers pulled back. Once again Elizabeth was left alone in the middle of an empty room in a dark, empty house—but this time she was breathing fast, her face was flushed, and her skin was tingling wherever his hands had touched her.

Frowning, she looked around the dark room.

"Tom? Tom, what are you doing? Why did you leave?"

From the other end of the house she heard the faint sound of a door closing gently, and then the dining room was once again awash in the pale, sickly light of the grimy overhead chandelier.

Soon Tom appeared, his hands black with dust and bits of cobwebs clinging to his thick brown hair.

Elizabeth stared at him, a quizzical smile frozen on her face. "That was fast," she said. "You just left a second ago."

"Really?" Tom raised his eyebrows and brushed at his hands in disgust. "It felt like it took an hour to find the cellar and wrestle with the fuse box. But the lights should be OK now. We definitely want a generator for the band, though. If they have powerful amps, it'll blow that ancient wiring to smithereens."

It's amazing, Elizabeth thought, lifting her hair off the back of her neck. *I'm standing here, practically on fire, my knees like jelly, and he's still Mr. Cool and Collected.*

"Hmm. Maybe it wouldn't be such a bad thing to have the fuse blow again," Elizabeth said softly, coming over to Tom and wrapping her arms around his waist. "Being here in the dark with you is kind of nice." She looked into his eyes and brushed a kiss across his cheek. He tasted a little dusty.

114

Tom smiled down at her and drew her close. In the faded dining-room light, his body felt familiar to Elizabeth—he felt like himself again. Tall, but not unusually tall. And he was solid—heavily muscled. "You mean maybe I could sneak a kiss?" he asked.

"*Sneak* a kiss?" Elizabeth chuckled. "Um, sure, if you want to call it that. That's one way of putting it."

Gently Tom lowered his head and kissed her. But somehow the unexpected, almost dangerous sense of magic was missing. He was Tom, and she loved him, and she loved kissing him. But it wasn't so overwhelming that it was almost scary, as it had been in the dark.

The cold light of reality, Elizabeth thought ruefully, kissing him back.

She tried not to show her disappointment as they separated, but she was surprised that Tom didn't seem more eager to repeat his searing, hungry embrace of a few moments before. *Maybe he's trying to be sensitive, for my sake,* she reasoned. *Oh, well.*

She gathered up her clipboard and looked around to see if there was anything she'd forgotten. Tom turned off the lights on their way out, and Elizabeth carefully locked the front door.

"I feel like I'm leaving something behind," she said, pausing before she took her key from the lock. "But I guess I have everything."

Tom smiled and put his arm around her shoulder as they walked to his car. Twice Elizabeth looked back at the old Hollow House, searching its dark windows for a light left on, or some sign that she should go back. But she didn't see anything. All the same, she had a strong sense of something being wrong. Almost as if someone was watching her, and she could feel his gaze reaching out, touching her.

In the passenger seat she stared at the house. She was being stupid. The whole party, the whole spirit of Halloween, was affecting her this year. She'd had such weird thoughts while Tom had been gone, and that nightmare . . . She shook her head and shivered slightly.

"Cold, sweetie?" Tom turned on the car's heater, then started to back down the narrow, unpaved driveway to the main road. The car's powerful headlights picked out the black silhouettes of the gnarled trees and threadbare bushes that surrounded the house. Dark shadows seemed to flit from tree to tree, surrounding the house. Elizabeth couldn't stop looking at it—she didn't want to turn her back.

"Everything OK?" Tom asked.

Elizabeth looked up and saw his eyes on her.

"Of course—I'm fine. I'm just hungry. Let's go straight to the cafeteria, OK?"

"Will do." Tom pulled the car out on the main road, and Elizabeth felt better, safer, now that they were under the streetlights. "You know, maybe you're a little tired—you've been working really hard at the station and spending all your spare time organizing this Monster Madness party." He reached out and took her hand. "Not to mention studying, paying attention to your needy boyfriend, and dealing with Jessica's soap-opera life."

Elizabeth smiled at his description of her life. He always knew the right thing to say to make her smile.

"Uh-huh," she agreed lightly. "I think it's the needy boyfriend that takes the most energy."

"Oh, you think so?" Tom asked teasingly.

"Yep."

"Good," Tom said firmly. "That's how it should be." He gave a small, self-satisfied nod, and Elizabeth started laughing.

Jessica stretched out on Elizabeth's bed and adjusted her twin's reading light. A stack of decorating magazines was piled up next to her, and a diet soda was perched on Elizabeth's night table. A manila folder of pictures ripped out of magazines was propped against the wall.

"OK, now," Jessica murmured to herself. "We're going with the leopard-print bedspread.

117

That's definite. But what to do about the windows?"

Jessica had been incredibly busy making inroads on her new room. She felt that she was definitely gaining ground over Alison Quinn in the battle of possession. After all, hadn't Jessica painted the room a nice cream color just that morning? It seemed to her that if one actually managed to paint the actual walls of a room, one should end up getting it. That was obvious. Of course, Jessica herself had only supervised the painting while she and Lila had sat and chatted. Three really nice guys from her physics class had taken care of the messy painting part. It had been really sweet of them. And all she had to do was promise a lunch here, a walk there, a movie. No problem.

Now that she had a blank, neutral canvas to work with, Jessica could get down to the nitty-gritty details. She'd ordered a new bed frame and mattress from a discount mattress place and charged it to Elizabeth. It would be delivered next week. She had gone for a double size. After all, she was a grown woman now. A babyish twin size was out of the question. New sheets, pillows, a comforter, and the all-important leopard-print bedspread were in huge bags all around the dorm room. She couldn't leave them at the Theta house yet. There was no telling what Alison might do.

Jessica clipped out a picture of a neat bedside table and added it to her manila folder. The door to the dorm room opened, and Elizabeth came in, almost tripping on one of Jessica's big bags.

"Hey," she said, grabbing a chair for balance. "How about keeping some of these things in the closet?"

"Won't fit," Jessica said, thoughtfully perusing a window treatment in *Mod Home* magazine. Then she looked up. "I'm glad you're here. I want you to look at some of the things I've been considering. Nothing is certain yet, but I've been milling around some ideas. Come see this room with a fake zebra carpet."

Elizabeth set her backpack on her desk and looked at Jessica. "How come you're not on *your* bed?"

Jessica met her eyes patiently. "Liz. *Look* at my bed. Now, I need feedback about accent colors. I'm thinking hot pink, with the occasional splash of gold and copper. What do you say?"

"I say clear some of this stuff off your own bed," Elizabeth said with a semiamused smile. She waved her hand, and Jessica followed the movement. Her own bed was in its usual chaos: unmade, covered with clothes, magazines, CDs, laundry in an uncertain, possibly washed state . . .

"Come on, Jessica," Elizabeth pressed. "Move 'em out. I want to study on my own bed."

After examining her sister intently for a moment and judging her unlikely to be cajoled, Jessica sighed and began to gather up her magazines.

"OK, OK, just a second." Jessica pushed everything on her bed down to the end, where it made a pile several feet tall across the width of the mattress. Then she settled herself on the bare sheet that was left. "Are you doing OK?" she asked Elizabeth with exaggerated concern. "You didn't fight with Big T, did you?"

"No, of course not," Elizabeth said with a smile, lying down on her bed. "Things with Tom are great. We just get closer all the time. It's just a chilly autumn night, and I had my heart set on snuggling into my own bed to study. I'm sorry to inconvenience you."

Jessica ignored Elizabeth's mock-conciliatory tone. "Maybe you haven't been sleeping well," she said, taking a sip of diet soda. "Last night you were actually talking in your sleep. I thought I'd have to set the room on fire again."

"Ha ha," Elizabeth said dryly. "Was I really talking in my sleep? How weird. I don't remember what I was dreaming or anything." Elizabeth propped herself up so she could see Jessica. "What was I saying?"

"Nothing interesting, I promise you," Jessica said in a bored tone. "Actually, I couldn't really understand much. Sometimes it sounded like you were talking French. Do you have a French exam coming up?" Jessica found a picture of a different kind of bedside table, and she ripped it out.

Across the room her sister nodded. "Yeah. I have to study for it tonight." She shrugged, a bemused expression on her face. "I didn't think I was that worried about it, but maybe I am."

"That wouldn't be unusual," Jessica said absently. "Hey! Look at this! What if I got a bunch of little pillows and piled them all up on my bed, like this?" She held up her magazine so Elizabeth could see the picture. "That is so cool, don't you think?"

"Jessica, you're forgetting something very important," Elizabeth said, sitting back and piling her pillows behind her. She opened her French textbook and got her notepad ready.

"What?"

"That effect only works when people can actually see the bed itself. In your case, it would be a waste of time." She gave Jessica a sweet smile.

Jessica's eyes narrowed. "Oh, very funny."

Chapter Ten

Elizabeth ran the tape of the ministory about Women Against Violence, the battered-women's shelter, she had prepared to air later in the week. It was late, past ten o'clock, and the WSVU offices were empty except for her. But this would be her only chance to put the finishing touches on the piece.

Tuesday. Not even Hump Day, she thought, rewinding the editing machine to run the loop again. It felt later in the week than that. Tomorrow she and Jessica would go to the Party Basket to buy most of the decorations and supplies they would need for Monster Madness. Thursday was clear, and Friday morning was reserved for the actual setup.

Thinking about the Monster Madness party made Elizabeth smile a little. It was going to be a fabulous party. Advance ticket sales had really taken off that week, and at five dollars a ticket, Elizabeth thought they would have a nice check to present to Women Against Violence. She felt proud of her fund-raising effort to benefit the battered-women's shelter.

Blinking, Elizabeth realized that she needed to concentrate again on the editing machine. Perhaps more coffee was in order. She stood up to head for the small, beat-up coffeepot that was the lifeblood of the WSVU office.

"Oh!" Freezing in her tracks, her eyes wide, Elizabeth stared at the tall, dark figure standing quietly just inside the station door.

"Y-you startled me," she stuttered, her eyes still locked on the stranger. A tiny chill skated down her back. Ever since the William White horror story, Elizabeth had been doubly on her guard with guys she didn't know. This man was tall and slender and seemed to be in his midtwenties or so. He was wearing black jeans, a black shirt, and some sort of foreign-looking black silk vest. But it was his face that made Elizabeth stand as if caught in the headlight of a train.

His face was pale in a way that Elizabeth had rarely seen in southern California. His eyes were a startling bright green—the green of wet leaves, of emeralds, of traffic lights. His hair was thick and as dark as night, brushed back smoothly from his forehead. Elizabeth had never seen anyone who looked quite the way he did. He was astonishingly, frighteningly handsome.

"I'm sorry," he said, in an attractive, melodious voice. "I didn't mean to startle you."

"Is there something I can help you with?" Elizabeth asked, drawing herself up to her full five feet six. *Look calm. Look in control.*

"Yes," the man said. His charming, male-model smile revealed shiny white teeth between firm, sensual lips. Elizabeth swallowed and forced herself to keep looking into his eyes.

"My name is Nicholas des Perdu," he continued. "I've come to Sweet Valley because of Tom Watts. I understood he works here, at this university TV station."

Whatever Elizabeth had been expecting, it wasn't this. Her mouth dropped open, and she shut it with a snap. Nicholas des Perdu! The world-famous journalist! Right here in the WSVU newsroom. Tom had told Elizabeth all about his weekend in New Orleans, but he hadn't described Nicholas des Perdu like *this*. In fact, he'd made Nicholas sound very talented and a little eccentric, but other than that, sort of unremarkable. There was nothing, nothing at all, unremarkable about the man standing in front of Elizabeth.

"Oh," was all she managed to get out; then she gave her head a little shake. "I'm sorry, I'm just very—surprised. But I'm thrilled to meet you." Elizabeth formed a professional smile, then stepped forward and held out her hand. When he shook it firmly, his eyes gazing into hers, she noticed how cool his fingers were.

"And I," came his cultured voice, "feel as if I've waited many lifetimes to meet you. Tom mentioned you to me when he was at my home."

Not knowing what to say to that, Elizabeth smiled a little and shrugged her shoulders. She held up her chipped coffee mug.

"I was just going to have a refill," she told him. "Would you like some coffee?"

"No, thank you," Nicholas said.

It was hard to stop looking at him, Elizabeth realized. It was as if all the knowledge of the world was contained in his beautiful carved-marble face. If she had the rest of her life just to sit and stare at him, she didn't think she'd be bored.

Elizabeth, for goodness' sake. What are you thinking?

To hide her confusion, she stepped back to her desk and sat down a little awkwardly. "Um, you said you were here because of Tom?" The wheels in her brain seemed to be moving in slow motion. She couldn't even remember what Nicholas had said when he'd first come in.

"Yes," the man said. He came closer to Elizabeth, though in her slightly bemused state she wasn't really aware of his walking. He sort of glided. Suddenly he was closer to her, close enough so that she could see the bright-yellow reflection of her desk lamp in his eyes. Then he sank gently, gracefully, onto the battered secondhand sofa that took up one wall of the room.

Elizabeth felt as if he were trying to memorize her. His gaze was like velvet fingers running over her skin, her cheekbones, her neck. And yet she didn't feel afraid.

"Yes, Tom asked me to look him up if I should ever be in Sweet Valley," Nicholas said. "And here I am. I thought I could consult with him further about the project he was working on." His eyes, locked on hers, seemed to spread a warm glow through Elizabeth's chest, down into her stomach. "But that isn't all I was looking for."

"No?" Elizabeth said faintly. Her hands rubbed nervously over the threadbare knees of her bleached jeans. She was painfully aware of her laundry-worn SVU sweatshirt, her hair pulled into an untidy ponytail with a rubber band, her makeupless face. *Great. I look like some stupid college kid, in front of one of the world's top news journalists. Why couldn't I have been wearing a suit, my hair in a chignon, looking fresh and intelligent?*

"No," Nicholas confirmed. "Let me explain. I was most impressed by Tom's hard work last weekend. His devotion to duty. He was amazingly hard to . . . distract."

"Oh, really?" Elizabeth nodded and tried to look professional. "Um, yeah, Tom really holds this station together," she offered. "He's taught me a lot."

"Indeed?" His ebony eyebrows rose in perfect arches. "Then perhaps you are the one I should be talking to. You see, I was so impressed with Tom last weekend that it occurred to me that he would be an excellent candidate for the Silver Quill award."

"The Silver Quill? I don't think . . . I haven't heard of that." An award for Tom! Obviously he didn't know about it—he hadn't mentioned a thing.

"It's an award that the CSNJ offers every year to a deserving intern," Nicholas explained. "The Conference for Southern News Journalists. It's not national, you understand, really only a local thing. But any student in America can be eligible, if they demonstrate the right qualities. Basically, it's a small statue of a silver quill"—Nicholas smiled charmingly, and Elizabeth felt the room's temperature rise several degrees—"along with a small scholarship, and the chance to choose his next summer internship from among several southern journalists."

"Wow, that's fantastic," Elizabeth said. "It

sounds incredible. Tom would be so happy—and no one deserves it more than he does."

"I'm glad to hear you say so." Nicholas put his long white fingers together thoughtfully. "Since you seem to know Tom well, perhaps you could help me."

"Oh, anything," Elizabeth promised, feeling excited and happy. "I would love to see Tom get that award."

"Well, I was hoping to learn more about Tom as a person—not just as a journalist," Nicholas said, leaning forward and looking into Elizabeth's eyes. "And it would be helpful to see some of the projects he's been working on—to get an idea of his interests, his work habits, the kind of stories he goes for."

"I could put some of his clips together," Elizabeth said. "He's covered some incredible stories so far this year. And he has a file of his newspaper work, too."

"Wonderful. I see you know exactly the kind of things I need. Now, I'd like to hear your views on Tom as person, as a . . . friend. I sense that you're close to him."

Feeling a tiny bit embarrassed, Elizabeth shrugged. "Yes—that's true. I'd be glad to tell you about him."

Nicholas looked down at the thin, elegant silver watch on his wrist. "It's rather late, I know, but do you think you could come have a drink with me? Or some coffee?" Again the charming, mesmerizing smile. "We might talk better in a more congenial atmosphere."

For a moment Elizabeth hesitated. After all, even though Nicholas des Perdu was a famous journalist, she didn't actually know him. But Tom had seemed to like him OK, she remembered. What did she think he was going to do? Kidnap her and hold her hostage? Anyway, he only wanted to talk about Tom. It would be selfish of her not to go.

"I'm not tired at all," Elizabeth said, standing up and clicking off her desk lamp. "A cup of coffee sounds great." She gathered up her backpack and shoved her purse inside. "Where should we go? Do you have any place in mind? There's the Coffee House on campus."

Nicholas smiled as he held open the station door for her. "Let's go someplace out of the way," he said.

The door opened at Tom's knock, and Jessica stood there in a silky robe. She was holding a magazine, and Tom was relieved to see that he wasn't waking her up.

"Hi, Jessica," he said, peering past her into the room. "I know it's late, but I haven't talked to Elizabeth all night. I was hoping I'd find her here."

"Nope," Jessica said, leaving Tom in the open door and going back to her bed. "I think she went over to the TV station." Yawning, she pushed her feet under the covers again, punched up her pillows, and settled back with her magazine.

"I checked," Tom said, feeling a little frustrated. "She wasn't there. She's not at the library, either. Maybe she's in Nina's room?" he asked hopefully.

Jessica shrugged. "Maybe. But it's kind of late to start dropping in on people. I mean, of course *I'm* awake. But a grind like Nina Harper probably hit the sack an hour ago, the better to rest all her overworked brain cells." Jessica grinned up at Tom.

"Huh." Tom thought for a moment. Where could Elizabeth be? He'd been studying in his room all night, then hanging out with his roommate, Danny Wyatt. But all of a sudden he'd had an overwhelming urge to see Elizabeth. Unfortunately, it looked as if it wasn't going to happen tonight. He became aware that Jessica was looking at him reflectively, as if wondering what Elizabeth saw in him. He and Jessica got along fine, but they didn't have much in common—nothing, really, except Elizabeth.

It always amazed Tom how completely identical the two girls were in looks, and how completely different they were in personality. Thank goodness. Because he thought Elizabeth was beautiful—he

130

thought Jessica was, too. But if he had to date Jessica, he would end up in a monastery.

"Anything else, Tom?" Jessica asked now, a little pointedly.

"No, no." He shook his head. "If Elizabeth comes back, just tell her I dropped by to say hello. Or she could call me to say good night, no matter how late it is. OK?"

"Okeydokey," Jessica said.

"Later," he muttered, and let himself out of their dorm room. In the hall he punched one of the walls in frustration.

Elizabeth, where are you?

Lisette.

Across the small marble table from him, Elizabeth was telling Nicholas a story about Tom Watts. From her hand gestures and facial expression, he could tell the story was meant to be funny, and he put a suitable expression on his own face. But he couldn't care less about Tom Watts.

Within him his blood tingled through his veins, making him aware of every inch of his flesh, every nerve in his body. The sight of Lisette, unchanged by time, fresh and whole and bursting with life, was almost too much for him to bear. For so long now he had been only half-alive. His existence was one endless, featureless night after another. He fed only out of need, never out of sheer appetite, never out of excitement. The years, the decades, the centuries, had slipped by him, not engaging him. But all that was going to change.

Now that he had found Lisette, he could start living again. Every night would be exciting, new. Every experience a fresh wonder, seen through her beautiful eyes. How he would delight in showing her his world. The nocturnal world, the world of power, the world of desire, the world of life everlasting . . . but first he would have to make her like him. He would have to give her the gift of eternal life.

Then he would never again have to fear losing her. She would never age, never die. She would stay forever as she was tonight: young, beautiful, her face unlined, her body firm and unmarred. Together they would roam the world, delighting in everything they saw, everything they did. It would happen soon, he promised himself.

"And then the police came," Elizabeth continued, taking another sip of her cappuccino. "But Tom had already pulled me out of the pit. And once I had calmed down, I realized that we . . . made a great team." She shook her head, and Nicholas watched in fascination as tiny golden tendrils curled around her face and trembled with movement.

Her hair is more golden than I remember. More sunlight, less moonlight. Her skin tone is warmer,

*more like a peach. Her curves are less extreme—her
arms have smoothly outlined muscles, where before
they were soft, like down.*

"It's an amazing story," Nicholas said softly,
edging his chair closer to Elizabeth's. "How terrified you must have been. Did you think you were
going to die?"

Elizabeth blinked, and he could see beyond her
eyes into her very thoughts. She looked down and
stirred her coffee.

"Yes, I guess I did think that," she said in a
voice so low only Nicholas's extremely sensitive
hearing could detect it. "If Tom hadn't rescued
me . . ." She took another quick sip, draining the
last of her cup.

"Death can be very frightening," Nicholas
whispered, reaching out to stroke her hand. Its
warmth, its smooth skin suffused with blood, almost made him lose control. "Or death can be
welcomed, like a friend. Like a lover." He lowered
his voice and Elizabeth bent closer to hear. "It all
depends on the circumstances." Turquoise eyes
were watching him blankly. He straightened up a
little. Better not go too far the first time. "But I
agree that life is a precious gift. It should be
guarded jealously, protected fiercely, never wasted.
And now, my dear, it grows quite late. You need
your rest. Allow me to see you home."

"All right." Her voice was subdued, her face

troubled. Nicholas's jaw ached, and he rubbed it, feeling the almost painful awareness of his teeth, sharp and waiting, cutting through his gums.

"I've enjoyed hearing about Tom," he said as they walked to the cafe door. "I'm beginning to get a very clear picture of who he is and what he means to you."

"Oh, good," Elizabeth said, the crisp night air smoothing her loose strands of hair back against her head.

"I have just two more requests." Nicholas took Elizabeth's elbow gently and led her to where his rented car was waiting. It was a low-slung black Lotus Elan, filled with coiled, eager power. He guided Elizabeth into the passenger seat, then shut her door behind her.

When he was in the driver's seat, he turned to her. The smoked windows dimmed the streetlamps to almost undiscernible orbs against the night sky. Inside the car it was dark and quiet and private. He used extreme willpower to keep himself from revealing the depths of his love right then. *It's too soon.*

"Two more requests?" Elizabeth's eyes looked a bit glazed, and her voice sounded thick. He let the outer reaches of his mind touch hers, ever so gently.

"Yes, my dear," Nicholas said. "One, I ask that you tell Tom nothing about the Silver Quill award—or about meeting me. Think of how much more surprised and pleased he will be if the award seems to come out of the blue."

"Yes, OK," Elizabeth said, looking through the windshield.

"And second, I want you to see me again so we can continue our discussion. I need more time to get the . . . information I need."

"I'm not sure I . . ."

Gently his mind reached out, and his consciousness guided hers.

"All right," she said. "When do you want to meet?" Her breath was soft and warm inside the small car.

"Tomorrow night. Is there a place we can be alone?"

Elizabeth nodded, a tiny frown marring her forehead. "Moon Beach. It isn't far from here. But no one would be there on a fall night."

Elation filled Nicholas as he turned the ignition key. This was going so much better than he'd hoped. With every passing moment he loved Elizabeth more, could see more of Lisette in her. Instead of being doomed to a meaningless lifetime spent drifting through eternity, he was actually being given a second chance. It was almost more than he could stand.

"Lovely," he whispered, looking at her profile. "Tomorrow night, then. We'll go to Moon Beach."

Chapter Eleven

"Ugh," Jessica grunted, pushing the natural wicker dresser into position along one wall. "Li, give me a hand here, will you?" It was Wednesday morning, and she needed to be leaving soon for her physics class.

Lila came over and helped push. "Is this where you want it?"

"Yeah." Jessica stepped back and brushed her bangs off her forehead. "I think it looks good there, don't you?"

"Uh-huh." Lila nodded, standing back to observe the whole room. "And you'll put the bed against that wall?"

"Yep. And guess what? I found this cool mosquito-netting stuff in a catalog. I'm going to hang it over the bed and let it drape down. Sort of an *Arabian Nights* effect."

Lila grinned. "You're really going all out, aren't you?"

"Absolutely," Jessica said proudly, leaning against the dresser. "I have to admit, it's put me over the limit on both of my credit cards, and one of Elizabeth's. But it'll be worth it. This room will be legendary in Theta history. If I'm going to be a major player in the sorority, I have to *act* like it—everything about me has to say it. Including my room. Especially my room."

"Is Elizabeth bummed that you're bailing on her again?"

"Not really," Jessica said. "Or at least she hasn't said anything. She knows how much I've been wanting to live at the Theta house."

"I guess setting her room on fire—with her in it—probably helped her see things your way," Lila said slyly.

Jessica made a face at her. "I didn't do it on *purpose*. And there was no real harm done," she pointed out. "Except, of course, to *my* brand-new leather jacket, which cost a fortune."

Lila laughed. "So there's only one problem, Jess," she said, examining some of the decorative touches Jessica had already strewn around. "This isn't exactly your room yet, is it? Not officially."

Jessica snorted. "Lila. Look around. Everything in this room is mine. I chose the paint color. I'm in the room. Alison doesn't have a chance."

"Does Alison know that?" Lila's brown eyes were shrewd.

Feeling impatient, Jessica shrugged. "I guess she'll find out when she sees all of my things. I mean, my new bed's being delivered on Monday. I'll be sleeping here that night. And that's only five days away, not counting today. What's she going to do?"

"I don't know," Lila admitted, running a hand over the pile of curtains they had yet to put up. "But it won't be pretty."

"Let's not talk about that loser," Jessica said crossly. "I'm sick of her."

"OK," Lila agreed with a grin. "Let's talk about my awesome costume for the Monster Madness party."

Jessica instantly felt better, and she plopped down onto her oversize black beanbag chair. "What are you going as?"

"Well," Lila began importantly, settling herself on the window seat. "The problem is, one has to look sexy and Halloweeny, *and* take into account any weather issues."

Jessica nodded sagely. "That's always the problem."

"And your basic witch doesn't really do it for me," Lila said. "But I had a brainstorm the other night when I was with Bruce."

"Yes?" Jessica prompted, resisting the urge to make any Bruce Patman jokes.

"Elvira, Mistress of the Dark," Lila said triumphantly. "Her costume is totally sexy. It's pretty easy to put together, it's kind of different . . . and I look fabulous in black."

"Wow," Jessica said admiringly. "That is a *great* idea." She nodded, picturing Lila in her costume. "That's going to be awesome. I can't wait to see people's reactions. Is your costume going to have Elvira's low neckline?"

Lila nodded with a grin. "Yep. I'm going to be the cleavage queen."

"Brilliant," Jessica said, laughing. "You're totally brilliant. I guess I'm still going as Catwoman—I have most of the costume together."

"We'll both be stunning. What about Elizabeth?"

"I don't know what she's going as. She and Tom will probably coordinate. I don't know. In the last day or two—"

"What?" Lila asked.

Jessica shrugged. "It's nothing. It's just once or twice lately she's been talking in her sleep. She says she's fine, and she seems fine, but . . . Last night she worked really late. This morning I tried to wake her to ask her if I could take the Jeep, and I could barely get her to open her eyes. And you know how bright-eyed and bushy-tailed she usually is in the morning. It's disgusting. But today I thought she was in a coma."

Lila raised her eyebrows. "When she talks, does she say anything interesting? Hot gossip? True confessions? Something telling us that she's been living a lie all this time?"

"Yeah, actually," Jessica said, looking wide-eyed and innocent. "It turns out she's been seeing Bruce on the side."

Lila threw a hot-pink pillow across the room. "So funny."

"Anyway, I don't know what her costume is going to be. You know how she and Tom are."

"Uh-huh. Peanut butter and jelly."

"Yeah."

"Tsk, tsk." Elizabeth couldn't help being a little appalled by Tom's files at the WSVU office. He had worked there two years, covering dozens of stories during that time, and they were all thrown into one big drawer. Not only was nothing labeled or dated or filed neatly, but his work shared drawer space with a spare coffee mug, several ancient magazines, and last year's calendar.

Elizabeth hated to imagine what his video files would look like. The only thing to do was take everything out and start sorting it, looking for Tom's best work, the pieces that would most impress Nicholas des Perdu. She glanced at her watch. At five she had a quick meeting with the decorations committee for the Monster Madness party. That should take only a half hour. Then, at seven, Nicholas was coming to pick her up.

Moon Beach.

Elizabeth's brow furrowed. Why had she agreed to meet him secretly? It seemed so unlike her. After all, she was completely devoted to Tom. But she couldn't deny that Nicholas was incredibly attractive. Unwelcome feelings of guilt came over her when she thought about him, and she tried to brush them away. He was so worldly, so sophisticated. He made her feel intelligent and witty and interesting. *More than Tom does? No. It's just different, that's all.* She knew why she was meeting him, she thought defiantly. Because she needed to give him information about Tom. Because she wanted Tom to get the Silver Quill award. She was really doing this for him.

Sighing, Elizabeth scooped out a big pile of Tom's clippings and carried them back to her desk. She got a newspaper ready to throw over the pile just in case Tom happened to come in.

There it was again. That feeling of guilt. She hadn't spoken to him at all last night. They *always* called each other to say good night, if they weren't actually together. Last night she had come home late and seen Jessica's scribbled note to call Tom, no matter how late it was. But she'd been tired, so she'd just gone to bed. And today she'd been, well, almost avoiding him. They hadn't eaten breakfast or lunch together, and Elizabeth had ignored his messages both at her dorm and here at the office.

I'll call him in a minute, she thought. *Right now I'm busy.*

First things first. Coffee. Much coffee is needed.

Elizabeth rinsed out her mug and filled it from the office pot. It tasted awful, as usual, but she found the bitter flavor reassuring. Tom had brought her back some coffee from New Orleans—French roast with chicory. It had been amazingly good.

Elizabeth settled down at her desk, trying to block out her officemates' chatter. It was Wednesday afternoon, and there were several people at the computer stations, or on the editing machines. For some reason Elizabeth was glad she wasn't alone, that it was daylight. She started sifting through Tom's stories.

It was easy to spot his early works. He'd covered things like pep rallies, sorority bake sales, charity car washes. But as Elizabeth began to put the articles in order, she saw how quickly he had improved. His stories became sharper and more focused, his investigative journalism more serious. He was really talented, she thought with pride. No wonder Nicholas wanted to nominate him for the award.

Nicholas.

For just a moment it was as if a cold breeze had

brushed across the back of Elizabeth's neck. She looked around but saw only the usual people doing the usual things.

"Elizabeth—there you are."

Elizabeth jumped at the sound of Tom's voice and quickly threw her newspaper over the stack of his articles. She really shouldn't have gone into his files without permission. Even if she was trying to help him.

"Tom, hi." Elizabeth smiled and held her face up for the kiss she knew was coming. Sure enough, her handsome boyfriend leaned down and kissed her. But it was more a quick brush across her lips than his usual warm and hungry embrace. She met his dark eyes and found them confused and a little hurt.

"Did you get my message to call?" he asked.

Guilt. No point in lying. Maybe just a little lie.

"Yeah, I did," Elizabeth said, sounding regretful. "I'm sorry." She waved an arm at her desk. "I wanted to get some work done, and then I was going to call. Sorry."

Tom looked down at her desk. "Looks like you're reading the comics," he said evenly.

"Oh, well . . . yeah. I'm just taking a five-second break," Elizabeth explained, a flush of embarrassment rising in her cheeks. "All work and no play, you know." She knew how lame her excuse sounded.

"It doesn't matter," Tom said, sitting on the beat-up couch by her desk. "Why don't we make plans for dinner? We could splurge, and instead of going to the cafeteria tonight, we could try that new vegetarian place on University Boulevard."

Sounds good, except I'm going to be with Nicholas. The very thought made a shiver of expectation run down her spine.

"Oh, gee, Tom, that sounds wonderful," Elizabeth said, thinking fast. "But I promised Jessica I would eat with her. She wants to go over some of the stuff for the party—you know, she's helping me set up for it. And she said she wanted to spend time with me now, since she's moving out soon." Elizabeth forced a laugh. "I think she feels a little guilty."

Tom's dark eyes regarded her steadily. "So you're having dinner with Jessica." It was a statement.

"Yeah." Elizabeth nodded her head ruefully. "But tomorrow night is open, and then on Friday we'll go to the Monster Madness party."

"Uh-huh."

Elizabeth could see Tom trying to be patient and understanding, and again she felt a twinge of conscience. He would thank her later, she knew, and they would laugh about it. But he didn't look too happy right now.

"Oh, well, I better let you work," he said, standing up. "I've got a class in a few minutes anyway. But, listen, I'll be home later tonight—why don't you call me, just to say good night?"

"OK," Elizabeth promised, giving him a big smile.

He leaned down again to kiss her good-bye, and Elizabeth felt the warmth of his mouth and his skin. Suddenly she wanted to grab him and leave the WSVU offices. She didn't care where they went—she just wanted to leave and to be alone with Tom and no one else. He was so solid, so strong, so warm. She didn't want anything to come between them.

"I miss you," he whispered, giving her one of his old smiles.

She wanted to burst into tears, but she didn't know why. "I miss you, too," she said. Then she watched him turn around and leave, waving at all the people who were greeting him. When he was gone and she looked down at her desk again, she felt bleak and old.

Chapter
Twelve

That witch. That unspeakable witch, Jessica fumed as she stomped across the campus quad. She had just finished unburdening herself over dinner with Isabella Ricci, one of her best friends, and she was still full of righteous indignation. Isabella agreed that Alison had gone too far this time.

After working on her room all morning and part of the afternoon, Jessica and Lila had taken a little break, walking over to the Coffee House for a fresh fruit shake. When they had returned, they found that Alison had done the unthinkable. She had taken down Jessica's curtains and replaced them with her own. Not only that, but she had pushed all of Jessica's furniture into a corner and covered it with a sheet. Then—and Jessica had no idea how Alison had accomplished it in less than an hour—she had actually pasted a wallpaper border all around the ceiling molding and the windows. A border, Jessica remembered with disgust, that did *not* coordinate with anything of Jessica's. And it was *pasted* up, actually *glued* to the walls. Now Jessica would have to rent a steamer machine to steam it off the walls. It was too much.

Jessica grimaced. Her dinner was sitting in her stomach like a lump, giving her a stomachache and making her irritated all over again. *Ooh, I could just kill her.*

"Jessica—wait up."

Jessica looked around and saw Tom Watts heading toward her from about twenty yards away. *Where's Elizabeth?* Jessica whined silently to herself, then felt bad about it. She shouldn't be mean to Tom—he was a great guy, and he made Elizabeth happy. Crossing her arms, she waited for him to catch up to her. It was just that he was so—nice. Not as nice as Todd Wilkins had been, though, actually, Todd had ended up being kind of a jerk, Jessica realized. But Tom was still sort of—*too* nice. What Elizabeth needed, Jessica reflected, was a little excitement. Not excitement like William White. But—*excitement*. Elizabeth needed a guy who would be unpredictable, who was different from anyone she'd known. Maybe someone older, someone with a wild streak.

"Hey," Tom greeted her, now that he was by her side.

"Hi, Tom," Jessica said, continuing to walk back toward Dickenson Hall.

"Did you just have dinner? I guess Elizabeth went to the library or something," he said, matching his steps to hers.

Jessica smothered a sigh. Tom was just so eager all of the time. Of course, Elizabeth was the same way about him. Just Tom, Tom, Tom, all the time. Tom this, Tom that. Fine. *Just don't put me in the middle.*

"Yeah, I just had dinner," Jessica said, trying not to sound pitying. "But I don't know where Elizabeth is. I haven't seen her since before dinner." Jessica looked up, struck by a thought. "Actually, you know, I thought she was with you. When I saw her, she was getting ready to go out."

"Out? Like on a date?" Tom's face was a study in barely repressed alarm.

"Well . . ." Jessica thought. It *had* looked as if Elizabeth was getting ready for a date. At least she'd been taking extra care with her appearance, which wasn't all that normal for Elizabeth. "I guess sort of like a date," she hedged, not wanting to get into an awkward conversation with him. "Maybe she was just tired of looking dowdy. Maybe she was just out of clean sweats and flannel shirts." Jessica shrugged.

"So you didn't have dinner with her?"

Looking at Tom's face in the glow from the

quad spotlights, Jessica tried to gauge his purpose. "No," she said slowly. "Was I supposed to?"

Tom shrugged. "Oh, just thought you might. No biggie. You don't know where she is now, right?"

"No," Jessica said, a trifle impatiently. "Why don't you two get each other beepers? That way you'll know where the other one is all the time, and I won't have to be anyone's social secretary."

Tom grinned, and just for a moment Jessica felt guilty about not being more helpful. "Sorry, Jess. I always just assume you have your finger on the pulse of SVU."

"Uh-huh," Jessica said grumpily, but Tom's placating words had their desired effect.

"Look, if you see Elizabeth, just ask her to call me, OK?" he said.

"Sure."

"Thanks." Another smile, and Tom veered off toward his own dorm, leaving Jessica looking after him. Was Elizabeth trying to get rid of him? Jessica knew her sister hadn't called him back. It was unlike her. Even when she was in the middle of being humiliatingly dumped by Todd, Elizabeth had still been polite to him. It was as if she couldn't be mean to anyone, no matter how justified it was. So what was going on with Tom?

Just ahead was Dickenson Hall. With any luck

Jessica would be moving out in five days. But first she had to take care of Alison.

A flash of golden hair caught Jessica's eye, and she instinctively turned to see who it was. Around the side of the dorm building, a long, low, totally amazing black car was parked. As Jessica watched, her interest piqued, she saw that the flash of blond hair had been none other than her own identical twin. Elizabeth, looking very much like Jessica, since she was wearing Jessica's oversize black sweater and black leggings, walked down the path to the car. The driver, someone tall and dark whose face Jessica couldn't see, stood by the car door, waiting. Elizabeth smiled at him, then climbed into the car. The door slammed, the driver assumed his own seat, and they roared off into the autumn night.

Well, jeez, Jessica marveled. What in the world was Elizabeth doing? Who was that guy? No one Jessica knew had ever had a car like that—not even Bruce Patman. And why was Elizabeth wearing Jessica's clothes? "Tune in tomorrow for the answers to these questions and others," Jessica quoted from her favorite soap opera. She let herself in the front door and headed up to their room, burning with curiosity.

Just when she was convinced she knew Elizabeth inside and out, her twin went and did something completely unexpected, Jessica mused, opening their door and collapsing onto Elizabeth's bed.

The phone rang, and Jessica groaned as she got up to answer it.

"Hey there," Lila said brightly. "Listen, Bruce and I are going over to El Capitano for a late dinner. Want to come?"

"Um," Jessica said, thinking. "Not really." After a whole lifetime of practically hating Bruce Patman, she was still a little disconcerted to see her best friend actually dating him. A whole evening spent in his company while he made dog eyes at Lila would be too much. "I just ate with Isabella. And Randy called earlier. He might come over for a while." Randy Mason, boy nerd turned Greek god, was a blast from Jessica's past that she was really enjoying.

"Oh, OK," Lila said. "Just thought I'd ask."

"Thanks anyway." She paused for a moment. "Listen, remember I said Elizabeth's been acting a little weird lately?"

"Yeah. So?"

"I don't know what's going on. She blew off Tom last night and today, but she's still moony about him, too. And I told you she's been talking in her sleep. Well, just now I saw her getting into a fabulous car with a guy I've never seen before. You don't think she could be two-timing Tom, do you?"

"Elizabeth?" Lila practically shrieked.

"You're right, you're right," Jessica said, shaking her head. "What was I thinking? I'm going to forget about it. You know what I really need to think about?"

"Getting that wallpaper border off the wall?" Lila suggested.

"Yeah, that's number one. But also, I need to get a carpenter out to the Theta house. I want to enlarge my new closet."

Inside Nicholas's Lotus Elan, was a separate world. The atmosphere was silent, dark, and dimly cool. The scents of leather upholstery, of wool carpet, of teak panels, surrounded Elizabeth like a welcoming glove.

Elizabeth looked down at Jessica's clothes, at her own hands clasped primly in her lap. *I'm not myself,* she thought. *I'm someone else.*

Since he had picked her up at school, Nicholas had been oddly silent. But it was a comfortable silence, full of shared glances, the quiet shifting of gears, the gentle purr of an incredibly powerful engine joyfully leaping down the highway.

Now Elizabeth sneaked a glance at him. He was casually dressed all in black, with a black cashmere turtleneck, black wool jacket, and black pants. His face was strikingly beautiful, his thick hair shiny, his eyes bright green and piercing.

And his smile was oddly white and infinitely compelling.

I'm doing this for Tom, Elizabeth insisted faintly to herself. Another thought followed. *I'm doing this for me.*

"It's a beautiful night," he said in his melodious voice. The sound washed over her like a gentle ocean wave, tugging her closer and yet pushing her back.

"Yes," she said. "Not too cold, not too hot." *There are a million things I should be doing right now. Homework, seeing Tom, cleaning my room, doing laundry, calling Nina . . .*

"Tonight let's pretend that nothing really exists," Nicholas said quietly, as if reading her thoughts. "Let's just enjoy the night air, the peaceful drive . . . and each other's company. I hope you're hungry—I've brought a picnic dinner."

Elizabeth swallowed, feeling as if the interior of the car were getting smaller. "That sounds great," she said.

Twenty minutes later they left the highway, and Elizabeth gave Nicholas directions to Moon Beach. As she had expected, on an October weekday night, it was completely deserted. Nicholas took a bundle and a basket out of the car's minuscule trunk, and together they walked in silence across the cool, pristine-white sand.

Beyond one of the lower dunes, Nicholas

153

spread out a soft wool plaid blanket. Elizabeth sat down on it, realizing she could no longer see the car; people driving by could no longer see them. They were in a private world, here by the ocean. Nicholas reclined beside her with easy, feline grace. Taking a bottle of red wine from the basket, he opened it and produced two wineglasses. Feeling awkward and gauche, like a schoolgirl, Elizabeth took hers.

There was a cool breeze coming off the water, but it was a mild night, and Elizabeth felt comfortable sitting on the blanket. The ocean was offering small, regular ribbons of waves—white-crested waves that spent themselves on the smooth sand and then were washed over by the next cycle. The sound was low and hypnotic, the air intoxicating.

"Drink your wine." Nicholas's voice was part of the wind, a force of nature that Elizabeth couldn't alter or deny.

She regarded her wineglass. She'd had wine before, but she was still underage, and it seemed exotic to be drinking on a school night. At least she wasn't driving. She took a sip, the full-bodied flavor bursting in her mouth like a piece of ripe fruit, then smiled up at Nicholas in surprise.

"This is wonderful," she said, taking another sip. "I don't usually like alcohol, but this is different."

Her companion smiled easily at her from the shadow of the dune. "I'm glad," he said. "It's a very old wine, very special. One of my favorites." He took a sip from his own glass, then pushed the stem down into the sand so it would stand up.

It felt completely natural for Nicholas to move closer to her on the blanket, and completely natural for Elizabeth to lean toward him. If they touched, it would be like touching moonlight. Nicholas was wiry and elusive and cool, without any of the heat or solidity Elizabeth was used to. They were sitting very close to each other, their legs brushing each other. Nicholas put his arm around her shoulders.

"Tell me about yourself," he said softly. "I want to know everything there is to know about you."

Elizabeth smiled at him, seeing his face half in shadow, half-illuminated by the moon, which was almost full. "There's nothing to tell," she said. "Anyway, I'm not the one being nominated for the Silver Quill award."

"No." Nicholas smoothed back a strand of her hair that had come loose in the breeze. "But to me you are still fascinating. I see a great deal of potential in you, Elizabeth Wakefield. A lifetime of potential. Many lifetimes of potential."

"Really?" Elizabeth felt herself relaxing. This scene was out of a fantasy, out of a dream. Nicholas des Perdu, one of the world's most noted journalists, was telling her she had potential, that he saw something special in her. Not only that, but she admitted to herself that he was darkly intriguing, an exciting older man who was arousing all sorts of feelings, unexpected and almost frightening, in her. One part of her brain was running through her usual reactions and warnings, but another part was being drawn inexorably toward him no matter what the consequences.

I always play it so safe, Elizabeth thought dreamily, gazing into Nicholas's deep-green eyes. *Why shouldn't I take a chance this once? Why shouldn't I do something just for me? I want to.*

There was no surprise, no fear, when Nicholas slowly leaned closer to her and took her chin in one of his cool hands. When Elizabeth set her glass down, it tipped over, spilling red wine onto the white sand. The liquid sank in immediately, leaving no trace except one tiny dot of dark maroon.

When Elizabeth felt Nicholas's cool lips pressing against hers, she sighed and closed her eyes. She felt as if she had been waiting for this all along, eager for it to happen, anticipating it. For her whole life.

Nicholas's kiss was sweetly familiar, Elizabeth thought as she put her arms around him and edged closer to his body. Everything about him, his scent, the way he felt, the murmur of his voice. She had experienced it all before. When he gently lowered her back onto the blanket, she didn't resist.

*　　　*　　　*

Tom slammed his fist down onto his desk at the WSVU station, causing Rachel Edison, a sophomore working on a news story, to jump about a foot in the air.

"Sorry, Rachel," Tom muttered.

"Something wrong?" she asked, her brown eyes quizzical behind her wire-rim glasses.

"No," he said shortly. *Nothing's wrong except that I might be losing my girlfriend, and I don't even know why.* Unwilling to believe that Elizabeth would actually go out with another guy behind his back, Tom had made every effort to find her, to give her a chance to explain. Maybe it was as Jessica had said. Maybe Elizabeth had just felt like dressing up a little. Apparently girls sometimes had those urges out of the blue. So Tom had checked the library, the Coffee House, the cafeteria, and the WSVU station. No luck.

Now, from his desk phone at the station, he had been making phone calls. He'd dialed Elizabeth's dorm room, Nina Harper, even Alexandra Rollins, though he knew that she and Elizabeth weren't that close. But no one had seen her. Elizabeth's own phone had rung and rung with no answer.

What was Elizabeth doing? What was wrong? Just a few days ago everything had been great. But it seemed as if ever since he'd got back from New Orleans, things had been weird between them.

With a feeling of dread Tom forced himself to remember the details of Marielle's almost-successful seduction. Had Elizabeth found out about it somehow? He didn't see how that was possible. There was no way he himself had let on about the experience, either by words or actions, and he never would. The whole thing was just a bad, creepy, embarrassing memory that he was determined to forget. But what was Elizabeth doing?

He wouldn't find her tonight, that seemed obvious. He hoped she would call him later to say good night, but he wasn't going to hold his breath. In the meantime maybe he could take his mind off things by immersing himself in work. He'd been planning to do an article about his New Orleans internship for the university newspaper. He might as well get started.

Chapter Thirteen

Pulling himself back from Elizabeth took the last shred of self-control that Nicholas possessed. Every sense was heightened, every cell in his body reeling with the memories of other kisses, other sighs, another woman in his arms.

Now he looked down at Elizabeth where she lay, her eyes still closed, against the darkness of the blanket. Her delicate nose and cheekbones were highlighted by the moonlight, making them look bloodless and finely carved. Slowly he traced their outline with one finger, and she opened her eyes and smiled dreamily at him. Her lips were swollen from their kisses, and her blue-green eyes looked glazed and content. She was beautiful.

His hand followed the curve of her neckline, down to where the top two buttons of her sweater had come undone. There. Her pulse, at the base of her neck. He could feel the life flowing through her veins, feel the throbbing pulse of young blood pumping beneath her flesh. His teeth began their familiar ache.

Soon.

He lowered his head again, his lips meeting hers, his fingers gently caressing the lightly tanned skin of her neck. Shutting his eyes, he allowed himself to think back to his first love, a love of so long ago—and to when he first became aware of the unbearable unfairness of mortality.

Back home to Chateau des Lys. Onward Nicholas urged his horse through the streets of Paris. Although it was late July, the weather was cold and rainy—a thin gray rain that coated everything it touched with an air of desolation, of loss. Nicholas didn't feel it. Around him, scattered through the streets, were signs of the battles that had filled the air with agonized screams and the heavy clang of sword against pitchfork. Up ahead, the grave digger's wagon was piled high with bodies, and Nicholas had to slow his horse to get by the narrow passage. The cloying scent of running blood, metallic and tangy in the heavy air, filled his nostrils as he edged past. But he was used to it.

Then he was barely a league from home; he could see the crenellated roofline of his chateau, peeking out from beyond the Cathedral of St. Anthony. Home, and Lisette.

He had been gone longer than he had anticipated, the time passing more slowly because of his longing for his bride. During the battles he had fought with ruthless efficiency, mindful only of the fact that the sooner he hacked his way through the uprising, the sooner he would be home with his beloved in his arms.

And now he was at his gate, then thundering up the drive of rutted wet clay. As he raised his fist to pound on his door, it was opened by an astonished footman.

"My lord!" he gasped. "But this is a miracle!"

"What do you mean?" Nicholas asked, kicking off his muddy, blood-caked boots and flinging aside his rain-soaked cape. He looked up and saw Jacques, who had been his faithful manservant since Nicholas had been a child, walk out from the kitchen.

"My lord," Jacques exclaimed. His beefy face was a mixture of joy and horror, his hands twisting nervously in his rough wool coat. "We are overjoyed to see you safe and sound, my lord."

"Where is my lady?" Nicholas demanded, starting to take the steps two at a time. "Lisette!" he bellowed. "Lisette!"

"Wait, my lord!" Jacques cried, standing at the bottom of the steps. "Please, I . . . have news."

"Make it fast, Jacques," Nicholas snapped, his head turned upward, waiting to see Lisette running down the stairs toward him.

"It's about . . . Madame des Perdu," Jacques said haltingly, giving the footman a nervous look.

Slowly Nicholas turned his head to regard Jacques. "What is it, Jacques?" He was aware of time stopping, slowing to a complete standstill as he came back down the stairs to stand in front of his manservant.

Jacques now looked as if he was cowering in terror. "Sir," he began haltingly, his voice hoarse. His red hands picked at the rough fabric of his clothes. "You see, sir, we thought—we got word that—"

"We thought you were dead," the footman blurted out, his thin face pale except for two patches of high color on his cheeks. "I swear, sir, we got notice that you had been killed at the Bastille."

"The Bastille?" Nicholas stared at him. "I was there, but it was no great battle. That was several days ago. Who sent word I was dead?"

"One of the field commanders, my lord," Jacques went on miserably. "A Monsieur de Tourney. I didn't know him, but he sent official word. There was no reason to doubt him. That was two days ago."

"We received a letter saying you had fallen at the Bastille," the footman repeated.

Nicholas shrugged. "You were misinformed. It is unfortunate, but no harm done. Now, where is my wife?"

"My lord," Jacques croaked, his heavy face lined with pain. "My lord, it was more than unfortunate. It was disastrous."

162

Nicholas stared at him, his green eyes like chips of arctic ice. A cold hand seemed to take hold of his heart, squeezing painfully. "Explain yourself."

For long moments Jacques was silent. His eyes rolled nervously, his face contorted with dread.

"Explain yourself!" Nicholas shouted in Jacques's face.

"My lord," he whispered, "naturally, Madame des Perdu learned of the letter we had received."

"The death letter," the footman clarified, nodding his head.

"She believed—we all believed—that you were dead. That we had lost our master." Jacques forced out the words as if they were choking him.

"Where is she?" Nicholas's voice was low and utterly controlled.

"She was . . . overcome with grief at your lordship's death," Jacques gasped.

"She—" the footman began, but couldn't continue.

"Where . . . is . . . she?" Nicholas's eyes bored holes into Jacques's fleshy face.

"My lord—she is . . . dead." Finally the words were spoken, and Jacques hung his head, as if expecting Nicholas to hew it off with his heavy sword.

The room spun around Nicholas. He blinked, gazing mindlessly at Jacques, at the footman, at the gilt plasterwork on the ceiling above him.

Obviously it could not be true.

"Where is my wife?" Nicholas asked calmly.

163

"She is in her chamber, my lord," Jacques whispered with bowed head.

Leaving his servants behind, Nicholas ran up the enormous curved staircase to the second floor. Down the hall he flew to Lisette's bedchamber, her own private sanctum. Without bothering to knock, he burst through the door. He expected with every fiber of his being to see her look up from her needlework, then burst into a dazzling smile at his safe return.

Instead he found Fantime, Jacques's portly wife, standing with a bowed head by Lisette's bed. She looked up, startled, then, in a grotesque mimicry of his fantasy, smiled in surprise at seeing her master, apparently miraculously brought back to life. Then she remembered and looked down, stricken, at the small, silent form lying on top of the bedclothes.

"Oh, master," Fantime said in a broken voice.

Crossing to the bed hung with heavy draperies, Nicholas stared down at Lisette. It was impossible that she was dead; she looked as fresh and beautiful as ever. They had made a mistake. She was only sleeping. But when he bent to kiss her lips, they were icy cold and unresponsive. Her hands, too, were cold and stiff; her eyelids refused to open.

"Master, she took her life, God forgive her," Fantime whispered.

"How?" His mind was screaming with pain; it seemed beyond his abilities to process what had happened.

"She took too much sleeping draft," Fantime said,

a tear rolling down her rough apple-red cheek. "Master, she was a good woman and true, and she couldn't live without you. I know God will forgive her sin and take her into heaven. You mustn't fear that."

That hadn't crossed Nicholas's mind, though of course everyone knew that to take your own life was a mortal sin. Even something as huge as a mortal sin seemed petty, inconsequential, compared to Nicholas's loss. If only he had come home two days sooner! If only that idiot de Tourney hadn't sent misinformation! If only Nicholas had refused to join the noblemen in their fight!

The pain was unbearable, the grief ripping through him like a tornado made of broken glass. Nicholas could not move from Lisette's bed, could not speak, could not see. He sat there, her small cold hand in his, until the sun went down.

The months following Lisette's death had been a blur. Broken, nonsensical images were all that he could recall. Here he was, attending Lisette's funeral, her pretty, small white coffin being pushed into his family's crypt. It had been a battle to have her buried on consecrated ground, because of her sin. It had cost a great deal. But Nicholas had no more use for his money.

An endless stream of friends and relatives had flowed through his house, wishing him well, praying for him and for Lisette's soul. Their faces had meant

165

nothing to him, their words had fallen on stony ground.

Afterward, alone, Nicholas had wandered the streets of Paris, unheeding of the fringes of unrest that still fomented on every street corner. It didn't matter. Let the people do as they would: His life was over. His title, his lands, his people, had no meaning without Lisette by his side. If he was reduced to one jacket and one ragged pair of breeches, that would be enough.

With methodical care he had worked his way through the wine cellar at Chateau des Lys, consuming bottle after bottle of rich burgundy. Fantime and Jacques had shaken their heads and whispered about him but hadn't dared try to interfere.

He had staggered through alehouses, through cheap bawdy-girl shows. His pocket had been picked too many times to count; he'd been beaten and rolled into the gutter. It had made him laugh. Now, looking back on it all, his pain phased to a dull-razor sharpness by time and distance, he could see that he had been courting death, that he had wanted to die. At the time, he had known only that he wanted not to think, not to remember.

It was a swirling, stuporous descent into darkness, into shame, into pain, into nothingness. And at the bottom of the well of nothingness, he was approached by a woman whose very name was pain, a woman who was a collector of souls.

One night as the moon sank toward the puddles

of mud in the street, as the first precursors of the sun's rays began to tinge the far horizon with pink, she collected his soul. It took only one embrace, an embrace that lasted for the rest of his life as a human, an embrace that didn't take long at all.

Nicholas didn't mind when he felt her sharp teeth neatly tear two pain-filled holes into his neck; he was so beyond physical pain or emotional discomfort that it barely registered. Nor was he aware of her tangled black curls spilling over his face, their scent of candle smoke, their texture of shipyard rope. Moments before, his hand had been on her arm, his fingers touching skin that didn't owe its whiteness to make-ups or powders, as was the fashion. Now his hand stilled as his fingertips picked up the steadily increasing drumbeat of her heart. He became aware, with an almost clinical detachment, that his own heartbeat was slowing, deepening, as her mouth became stained red with his life's blood.

His eyes met hers. With a grin he realized he had drunk too much fortified wine—why, he had hardly any sensation at all in his limbs. A languorous stillness settled over him, like a silk comforter, and he felt the earth's weight pool in his body. He was floating. He was too heavy to move. Some tiny corner of his brain seemed to spark then, as her black eyes smiled down into his. He felt the last, frantic fluttering of his mortal soul as it beat within his chest. He knew then that he was dying, and that he would soon be with his beloved, either in heaven or hell. That thought caused him to smile, and he closed his eyes, his bloodless hand dropping to the ground by his side.

When he woke again, he was in a coffin.

When he realized that in fact he wasn't dead, was in fact condemned to a soulless, deathless life for all eternity, his screams of rage caused dogs to start to howl as far away as three miles.

"I'm sorry, my pet," the woman said evenly as she performed her toilette at a gilded mirror deep in the ancient catacombs of Paris. Calmly she regarded him, regarded his rage, as she twisted her black curls over two fingers. "But you were much too pretty to let die." She turned to face him, her features expressionless, her eyes unfathomable. "Come, now, don't be bad. You'll like it, you'll see."

She had smiled, the mistress of pain, and with her sharp thumbnail had punched a spurting gash beside her breastbone. The blood, dark as old wine, warm as tea, spilled across her white skin and down the gathered, rigid lace of her corset. That was all it had taken. Like a marionette on strings, the smell of that blood—acrid, tangy, metallic—had pulled Nicholas forward until he sank to his knees before her. Hating her with all his being, hating himself, he fastened his lips to the wound and drank. She stroked his hair and soothed him, murmuring encouragement, laughing at the first dull, tentative pressure of his newly sensitive teeth.

Some time later Nicholas emerged from the dark-ness knowing that he had changed from prey to hunter, and he would hunt forever, and his pain would continue until the end of the world. The knowl-edge filled him with unimaginable horror. His new powers, his limitless strength, his new hungers and needs, would not comfort him for a very long time.

Oddly enough, it was the tiny, wind-borne rus-tle of dune grass that made Elizabeth open her eyes. As if she had just woken from a deep, drug-induced sleep, she looked around, startled, and re-alized to her horror that she was lying on a blanket on the beach with Nicholas. And she was kissing him.

What's going on? she wondered with panic. Her hands pushed at Nicholas's chest, and he, too, opened his eyes and drew away from her a bit.

"Are you cold, my darling?" he asked in his honey-smooth voice with its faintest touch of an accent.

My darling! I'm not his darling! Oh, no.

"No, no," Elizabeth muttered, struggling to sit up. She pushed Nicholas away more forcefully, and he instantly let her go and sat up beside her. Her face blushed furiously as she realized that a couple of her sweater buttons were undone, exposing her throat. Quickly she fumbled with the buttons, but her hands felt thick and clumsy.

"Wait," Nicholas said kindly, seeming to understand her distress. He moved her hands away and efficiently fastened her buttons again. Then he smiled beautifully at her and brushed a strand of hair away from her face. "Are you all right? Did I do something wrong?"

His voice was infinitely understanding and attractive. Elizabeth's fears dissipated immediately.

"No, Nicholas, it isn't that," Elizabeth said, pushing back her hair, which had come undone from its sophisticated knot. "It's just—I guess I suddenly realized what I—what we were doing. I'm not ready for it." She turned her head away so he wouldn't see her feelings of regret. *Tom.*

If Nicholas felt impatient or disappointed, he didn't show it. Instead he rubbed her shoulders in a comforting way, then packed up their basket. When he stretched out one fine, long-fingered hand, she had no hesitation about taking it.

"I'm sorry, Nicholas," Elizabeth said as they crunched back over the glittering sand to the car. "I didn't mean to ruin our evening."

"Time spent with you could never be a disappointment," Nicholas said. "And we have lifetimes to get to know each other. Please don't worry yourself."

But Elizabeth did feel worried, all during the long, silent ride back to Sweet Valley University. For the first time in her life she felt torn in two directions, and she was scared about what her choice would be.

"Pretty dead in here, huh, sweetheart? But it's only Wednesday."

Nicholas judged the woman to be in her late thirties, although in this lighting and with that much makeup on, he knew she could pass for thirty-two or so. She was a common enough looking woman—fairly attractive, though the innate freshness of youth had faded, and the harsh light of disappointment shone in her eyes.

Nicholas looked at his watch and took another sip of his drink. "Actually," he said in his cultivated tone, "it's Thursday now."

The woman seemed to think this was the funniest thing she had ever heard. Nicholas smiled at her laughter.

"What are you drinking?" he asked.

For just a moment her bravado faded, and her eyes sharpened as she weighed Nicholas's pros and cons. He knew she found him attractive; most people did.

That was one thing. It was another thing to go a step further, to let herself become beholden to him by his offer of a drink. He could hear her mind working, its edges dulled by other drinks, by the bar's smoky, alcohol-scented air. Finally she decided that one drink was harmless.

"A seabreeze," she said.

It was funny, Nicholas thought as he gave her order to the bartender. Now that she had taken that step, she was looking at him almost shyly. He moved his stool over next to hers and put money on the counter. When the bartender came back, Nicholas faded into the shadows of the room. He knew the bartender would never remember him.

"My name's Sheryl," the woman said as she sipped her drink. "I got a raise today. That's why I'm celebrating."

"Congratulations," Nicholas said, toasting her with his own drink. "Today is your lucky day." As they sipped their drinks, he noticed the deeply tanned skin of her neck. Everyone was tan here. It seemed unnatural, somehow. Nicholas preferred pale skin, skin that looked untouched. He wondered if Elizabeth's coloring would fade, once she no longer saw the sun. He thought it probably would. Then she would be even more beautiful, if that were possible.

With his razorlike vision he could see the sun damage on the skin of Sheryl's neck. A dangerous thing, the sun. It wasn't obvious now, but in a few years Sheryl's lines would deepen, the skin would thin out, spots would appear. But she wasn't going to have to worry about that.

Chapter Fourteen

"Want some more juice?" Tom tried hard to keep his voice neutral. Across the cafeteria table from him, Elizabeth was working on her Spanish omelet.

"Thanks, that would be great." She smiled up at him, and he felt more confused than ever.

As he filled their juice glasses, Tom reviewed the situation. Elizabeth had been avoiding him, not returning his calls. He had no idea where she had been last night or the night before. Now they were having breakfast together, the way they usually did, and Elizabeth seemed, if not totally normal, at least not as if she hated him. He felt as if he were losing his mind.

When he returned to their table, he found that they had been joined by Nina Harper. The girls were talking about the Monster Madness party.

"I've got some errands to do in the morning, but I'll meet you at the old Hollow House tomorrow at ten A.M. sharp," Nina was saying. "We'll decorate, set up the tables, and put out the drinks and stuff."

"Denise, Jessica, and one or two other people are going to help, too," Elizabeth said. "I think we'll be able to get it ready in time."

"Are you going to help, Tom?" Nina asked, taking a sip of her coffee.

"You said you would," Elizabeth reminded him.

Tom felt frustrated. *He* wasn't the one going around breaking promises. "If I said I would, then I will," he said pointedly. "I don't say one thing and mean another."

Across the table, Nina's brown eyes flicked quickly between Tom and Elizabeth. A slight look of alarm seemed to cross her face as she took in Elizabeth's blush of embarrassment and Tom's steady resumption of his breakfast. Quickly she drained her coffee cup, grabbed her backpack, and stood.

"Well, guys, I'll see you tomorrow morning, if not before," she said with artificial brightness. "I better get to chemistry. See you later."

"'Bye, Nina," Elizabeth said faintly.

Tom forced a smile and a wave.

For a few minutes he and Elizabeth ate in silence. Tom thought she looked pale and a little tired. *What should I do?* Should he confront her now? He hated the idea that he had become a possessive nag. Elizabeth had never given him reason not to trust her before. On the other hand, she had never acted like this before.

"So do we have anything to talk about?" he said finally.

Elizabeth looked up. "What do you mean?"

"I mean, is there anything going on that we should discuss? Anything about us?" Tom tried to sound casual and nonchalant. He didn't want to scare her off—didn't want her to see how torn up he was.

Elizabeth shook her head and smiled at him. "No," she said evenly, shaking her head. Her blue-green eyes met his, and she reached across the table and patted his hand. "No, everything's OK. Right?"

It almost sounded as if she were trying to convince herself as well as him, Tom thought. Having prepared himself to be calm and nonjudgmental, no matter what she told him, Tom was left sort of empty-handed at Elizabeth's answer.

"Right," he said slowly, weighing his options, which seemed to be dwindling by the second. "Well, how about a movie tonight, or dinner? I know it's only Thursday, but . . ."

"Yeah," Elizabeth said, nodding. "That would be great. You mentioned that new vegetarian place—we could try that. And what's playing at the University Quad?"

"Um, I think it's a revival. Since it's so close to Halloween, it's probably a horror movie. I'll find out, and we can decide over dinner." Tom suddenly felt lighthearted and happy. A whole evening with Elizabeth—something he used to take for granted. He almost felt as if they were going on their first date all over again. He gave her a big smile. "I'm really looking forward to it."

"Me, too." Elizabeth smiled back at him and finished her juice.

"Yo! Ms. Mysterious! Wait up."

Elizabeth turned and shielded her eyes from the sun. Jessica was hurrying toward her across the quad, her blond hair flying, cateye sunglasses perched on her nose.

"Isn't this sunshine great?" Jessica greeted her. "I feel like it's been cloudy for days."

"It hurts my eyes," Elizabeth said.

"So wear sunglasses," Jessica said, pointing toward her own. They walked in silence for a minute toward the humanities building.

"Well?" Jessica finally prompted her.

"Well what?" For some reason Elizabeth didn't quite feel up to dealing with her sister that morning.

It had been a relief to come home last night

and find Jessica asleep before her. She felt so confused about her growing feelings for Nicholas—especially since she knew she still loved Tom. The whole world seemed a little topsy-turvy.

"Last night I saw you getting into the coolest car I've ever seen," Jessica said impatiently. "With some tall, dark stranger. And you were looking very slinky and Jessica-like, since you were wearing some of my clothes. Not to mention the fact that Puppy Eyes has been calling at all hours, trying to find you. Honestly, even *I'm* almost embarrassed at the way you're blowing him off."

"I'm not blowing Tom off," Elizabeth responded. "Good grief, it's not like we're joined at the hip. It's not a crime if twenty-four hours pass without our talking."

"*I* know that," Jessica said dramatically. "And the rest of the world knows that. But you and Tom have never seemed to know that. In fact, you two have always been so repulsively huggy-kissy that most of us have given up on you completely. Now *one* of you—the blond one—seems to have changed your tune. *Plus* a tall, dark stranger has suddenly arrived on the scene. Coincidence? I don't think so." Jessica shook her head, and her long blond hair swung back and forth.

Elizabeth sighed. When Jessica put it like that, Elizabeth had to admit her sister had a point. Which was frightening in and of itself. Combined with how confused she felt, especially when she was with Nicholas, it was as if she were being sucked into a completely alternate universe. And yet she didn't want to tell any of this to Jessica. Usually she and her twin confided in each other about anything and everything. But this was all so new, so strange, and so nebulous, somehow . . . it was hard to put her finger on exactly what she was thinking and feeling.

"Just answer the question," Jessica said crisply. "Who was the hunk with the unbelievable car? And if you don't want him, can I have him?"

"Jessica! Look, he's not—anybody. He's someone I'm working on a story with, that's all. It's not a big deal," Elizabeth lied. "And no, you can't have him. Jeez."

"Hmm." Jessica looked unconvinced, and Elizabeth thought with a sigh that she would no doubt bring up the subject again later.

"So what's with Tom?" her sister pressed.

"I've just been really busy this week," Elizabeth defended herself. "If you must know, the story I'm working on sort of revolves around Tom. In a good way."

"Yawn. OK, fine. I'll let you go for now, but don't think you're off the hook. I saw what you were wearing last night. Now, two things."

Elizabeth didn't try to conceal her sigh.

Jessica ignored her. "Number one, I want you

to come to Theta soon and give me advice about the room. Wait till you see what Alison Quinn has done."

Elizabeth nodded. "Fine. I can do that."

"Number two is that while you're out wearing my clothes, gallivanting around town in the dark with strangers, please be careful. I just read in the paper this morning that a woman from a local bar was found murdered."

"Murdered?"

"Uh-huh. And get this. She'd been bled to death, like from a vampire. Can you believe it? Talk about sicko." Jessica shuddered. "I gotta run. I have some class now." Jessica flipped open her Filofax and checked the date. "Some class in . . . room one-thirteen. See you later."

"'Bye," Elizabeth said, watching her sister stride purposefully away. For some reason the news of the local murder made her feel profoundly strange and nervous, as if the sun had been suddenly blotted out. But she had no idea why.

"So when are we supposed to clean his room?" Marisol tapped her foot impatiently and glanced at her watch.

"I don't know," Theresa answered grumpily. She checked their schedule. "This floor has to be done by one thirty. How long has that Do Not Disturb sign been there?"

179

Behind the two housekeepers, the elevator doors opened, and automatically Theresa pushed their cleaning-supply cart to one side to make way for the hotel guests. A young porter, wearing the maroon-and-gold uniform of the Sweet Valley Grande Hotel, pushed his luggage dolly down the hall. A middle-aged man and woman followed him.

After they had passed, Marisol met Theresa's eyes. "What are we going to do?" she asked in a low voice.

"What did yesterday's crew do?" Theresa asked. Although she was the head housekeeper for the west wing of the Sweet Valley Grande, she had been off yesterday and another crew had done that floor.

Marisol looked worried. "They skipped his room, I think. Later, during dinner, they tried again, but he had his dead bolt on."

Theresa's dark eyes widened, and she put her hands on her hips. "Has anyone been in his room since he got here?" she demanded.

Marisol shook her head. "Not that I know of. On Wednesday I tried again, after I was off duty, just to give him some fresh towels. But he wouldn't let me in."

"What about a passkey when he's not there?"

Shrugging, Marisol said, "He's always there. His dead bolt is on. It's weird—what's he doing in there? Is he a drug dealer or something? If he wants to sleep all day, fine. But what's he doing at night?"

"Is he famous?" Instinctively Theresa mistrusted celebrities. They always made the most demands, and the biggest mess, then left the smallest tip.

Marisol shrugged. "Don't know. He has a weird name. I've never seen him."

Precious minutes had ticked by while they debated the thorny problem of the mysterious guest in suite 1227. Theresa had to make an executive decision.

"Let's skip his room for now. This afternoon I'll talk to Ms. Wilcox about it and see what she says." Ms. Wilcox was the general manager of the Sweet Valley Grande. She would know what to do, and her word was law. Already Theresa felt better.

Marisol giggled as they moved their cart down the hall to the next suite. "I just hope we don't find any dead bodies in there after he leaves."

Theresa made a disgusted sound and shot the younger woman a warning look. "Don't laugh," she said. "You don't know the kinds of things that happen at these fancy places."

"I got my horse right here, his name is Paul Revere," Jessica sang as she pulled her Jeep into the driveway of Theta house.

"What's that you're singing?" Randy Mason asked, getting out of the passenger side.

"*Guys and Dolls,* silly," Jessica said, opening up the back of the Jeep. She gave Randy an affectionate glance. Throughout grade, middle, and high school, Randy Mason had been the geek extraordinaire of her class. "Science Nerd" had been written all over his freckled face, and his red hair and glasses had rounded out the picture. Jessica had never really disliked him or been all that mean to him, but when anyone needed an example of someone with the least romantic potential, Randy's name had always come up.

What a difference time could make, Jessica marveled as she pulled her sleeping bag out of the back of the car. She dropped it onto the ground and handed Randy a lamp and a wicker magazine holder. "Here. Thanks."

Time had in fact been very good to Randy. Once a pale, reedy little beanpole, he had grown to over six feet, with a muscular, athletic body. Bright-red hair had darkened to a deep auburn, and contacts had replaced his glasses. Even his freckles had faded. Now he was adorable, gorgeous, hunky. And, naturally, here he was, crazy about Jessica. She was more than willing to have him totally crazy about her.

"OK, now, let's get this stuff to my new room," Jessica told him as she opened the front door of Theta house. Shifting the sleeping bag to one hand, she led Randy down the hall. She waved to her fellow Thetas, calling greetings and enjoying the admiring glances directed Randy's way.

"This room is going to be *so* great," Jessica told Randy as she paused in front of the back-parlor door. "It's big, it's a single, and it's on the first floor." She gave him a flirtatious glance and was rewarded by the sight of ardor leaping into his eyes. "It'll be completely private."

Randy grinned.

"Ta da!" Jessica threw open the door with a dramatic gesture.

"Wow," Randy said, sounding surprised.

Jessica frowned at him, then looked into the room. "Oh, my gosh!" she screamed, running inside. "That jerk! I can't believe she's done this! She's ruined everything!"

"What jerk is that?" Randy asked, looking around.

"Alison Quinn," Jessica seethed. "She still has the pathetic misconception that she'll end up with this room. But she is so wrong."

"Hence the sleeping bag?" Randy guessed.

"That's right," Jessica snapped. "And obviously I'm not a moment too soon." While Jessica had been away, Alison had hung chintz valances over the windows. Lacy panels screened the room from the yard. Jessica's things had again been pushed into a corner and covered with a sheet. An old-fashioned flowered hooked rug filled the center of the room, and a bentwood rocking chair was nestled cozily in one corner, a reading lamp by its side.

"I take it Alison's taste is different from yours?" Randy questioned timidly.

"Different! Look at this place," Jessica wailed. "It looks like Laura Ashley came in here and threw up. No, my stuff is so much cooler."

Randy moved closer to her and put a strong arm around her back. She felt his warmth through her cotton sweater and the hardness of his chest against her side.

"Come on, Jess," he said in a husky voice. "Let's ditch her stuff and get your things put back where they belong. Then you'll feel better. OK?"

He really is the sweetest thing, Jessica thought. She put her arms around his neck and drew him closer, then pulled his head down for a kiss.

"Sounds good to me," she whispered.

Chapter
Fifteen

"Come here, my precious."

Up on the small movie screen at the university movie house, a tall, dark man wearing a flowing cape beckoned to the blond heroine. She batted her eyes, seemingly mesmerized by his voice. She was in her nightgown, and her arms were stretched in front of her as if she were sleepwalking. Slowly she swayed toward him, and he caught her gracefully over his arm.

A few rows ahead, some frat guys snickered.

Elizabeth squirmed in her seat, feeling Tom's arm draped over the back of her chair. She picked up the diet soda at her feet and took a long sip. It was hot in the theater.

The man on the screen bent over the woman, as if to kiss her. But at the last moment his mouth opened, revealing pointed, shiny white fangs. The woman's eyes fluttered shut, and the man swooped, sinking his fangs into her white-skinned throat. A thin, dark trickle of blood ran down her neck. She didn't seem to care.

The frat guys snickered again, and two of them got into a small popcorn war.

Elizabeth fidgeted in her seat again. *I'm really not enjoying this.* Next to her, Tom was frowning at the screen in concentration, seemingly unaware of his surroundings.

The movie was an old one from the forties, and the special effects were dated and hokey. However, the audience seemed to be totally into it, the girls screeching at the scary moments, the guys making sound effects of their own, yelling out editorial comments.

But Elizabeth felt extremely uncomfortable watching it. She suddenly realized how much she wanted to leave.

Tom was still frowning at the screen, where two policemen were investigating the death of the heroine. With his spare hand he was methodically eating popcorn from the monster-sized bucket they had bought.

"Tom?" Elizabeth whispered. He leaned closer to her but didn't look at her.

"Tom." She jostled his arm.

"Huh? What?" he whispered back.

"I don't like this movie. Could we go? Maybe do something else?"

"What? What do you mean?"

Impatience flowed through Elizabeth like an electric spark. "I don't like this movie," she said more forcefully. "I want to go. Do you want to come with me?"

"What? You want to go?"

Blowing out her breath in exasperation, Elizabeth grabbed her jean jacket and got up, stepping over people's feet to get to the aisle. Once clear, she stormed up the aisle and pushed through the doors into the brightly lit lobby. She already felt better. That whole movie had given her the creeps. It was unbelievable what people were willing to sit through, she thought, shoving her arms into her jacket. Vampires. It was so stupid.

Unbidden, Nicholas's face appeared in her mind. She knew he would have hated this movie, too—he was obviously much too sophisticated to enjoy a ridiculous old movie like this. What was he doing tonight? Was he trying to call her? With a growing sense of disquiet, Elizabeth realized she missed him.

The doors swung open behind her, and then Tom's hand was on her shoulder, making her jump.

"Liz, what's wrong?"

"Nothing," she said, scrambling to collect her thoughts. "I just thought that movie was dumb. I didn't want to waste any more of my time. But you can stay here and watch it if you want. I don't want to ruin your evening." *I seem to be saying that a lot lately,* she thought ruefully.

Without waiting to see if he would follow her, she went out into the night, then turned left toward the quad and Dickenson Hall.

"Hold on a second," Tom said, catching up to her. "Fine. We don't have to see the movie if you don't want to. I thought it was kind of . . . I don't know. I wasn't enjoying it either. But I'll take you wherever you want to go—I don't want you walking anywhere by yourself." He smiled at her and put his arm around her shoulder. Elizabeth immediately felt rude and ill-tempered.

"Why not?" she asked.

"There have been a couple of local murders lately," he said, his voice sounding tighter. "Some kind of creep is stalking this area."

"Jessica told me about one woman. Was there another one?"

Tom nodded. "Yeah, from last Tuesday, except it was a guy who was killed. A young guy. I just saw it in the evening paper, when the cops linked the two deaths. It's probably just a coincidence, but all the same, I'd feel better if you weren't alone. So what do you feel like doing?" he asked.

Overhead the moon was waxing—tomorrow, the night of the Monster Madness party, it would be full. The sky was clear except for shredded wisps of dark clouds racing across the sky. As they walked down the dark, silent sidewalk, the leaves of the trees above them rustled. Elizabeth felt jittery, as if someone was watching them, or as if she was about to walk into danger.

But not with Tom. With Tom you're as safe as you can be.

She took his hand in hers and rested her head against his shoulder. If only everything was as it had been last week. If only nothing ever had to change. If only she had never met Nicholas. Tom gently stroked her hair.

"We could go get some coffee and dessert," he suggested. "Or . . . we could get some coffee and take it back to my room. Danny's out with Isabella tonight."

Elizabeth knew what that meant. Did she feel like going back to Tom's room? Not really. She always loved kissing him, but tonight for some reason she just didn't have the energy. The scene played itself through in her mind. They would kiss for a while, snuggling close, one of them would decide they were getting into dangerous territory, they would pull back, and so on and so forth. The usual. She just wasn't up for it.

"Actually, Tom, maybe I should just go home. Jessica's staying at the Theta house tonight, and this is my chance to catch up on my sleep. I feel like I could use it."

"Are you sure you just want to go home?" Tom sounded disappointed.

"Yeah." Elizabeth nodded. "Sorry. I know it's not much of a date."

"No, it's all right. No biggie."

They cut across the quad in the dark. Several groups of students were hanging out under the trees, although it was slightly chilly. Elizabeth could hear their muffled voices and the occasional sound of laughter. At Dickenson Hall she paused by the front door.

"Should I come in for a minute?" Tom asked, his dark eyes looking into hers.

Elizabeth forced herself to shake her head regretfully. "I'm really tired, Tom. I'll just go up and get into bed. I'll call you tomorrow, OK? Or I'll see you at breakfast. And then we can go over to the old Hollow House together."

Tom looked as if he wanted to say something but had decided not to. Instead he nodded, then took her gently in his arms and kissed her. It was a brief kiss, soft and sweet, not like their usual passionate good-byes. Elizabeth felt very sad.

Then he turned and was gone, loping down the path that led to his own dorm. When he disappeared into the shadows of the night, Elizabeth pulled open the glass double door and went inside. What was wrong with her? Why couldn't she get Nicholas out of her mind?

*   *   *

From where he blended with the blackest shadows of a tree, Nicholas watched Elizabeth and Tom kiss. Then Tom walked away alone, and Elizabeth went inside, looking sad. A minute later a light went on in the window Nicholas knew was Elizabeth's.

Lisette, he thought, *why have you betrayed me with another?*

Elizabeth was walking alone through a dark woods. It was nighttime, and she was in a long, old-fashioned, flowing white gown. Loose blond hair swirled around her head, whipping into her eyes and mouth. The leaves and sticks beneath her bare feet were damp and slick with rain. Branches reached out to her, snagging the fabric of her dress, tangling in her hair.

Where was she? Why was she here? Her eyes searched the trees futilely for some sign of life—a light, a dwelling. But everywhere was blackness. Overhead, owls swooped in the night sky, hooting eerily. Before her, things skittered along the ground.

Elizabeth saw gleaming yellow eyes deep in the blackness. They blinked slowly and disappeared.

A cold trickle of fear began to creep down her back. The chill wind raised goose bumps on flesh, and she wrapped her arms around herself.

Where can I go for help? It felt as if she had been walking for hours but not making any progress. For all she knew, she was going in big circles, losing herself deeper and deeper in the woods. Now branches were scratching her arms, and each little cut stung and burned.

Elizabeth was close to tears. Stopping for a moment, she stood in a tiny clearing. The trees seemed to be closing in on her. Dawn was interminable hours away. There was only a thin sliver of a pale moon, barely enough to illuminate the trees and turn them into black and threatening figures.

Then she heard footsteps, distinct footsteps, coming toward her across the wet leaves. A gust of cold wind blotted the sound for a moment, but when Elizabeth strained her ears, she could hear them again. Was it an animal? The steps didn't sound stealthy enough. No, it was a person. Every muscle in her body was tightly wound and cramped with fear. Panic rose like bile in her throat, and she put her hand over her mouth so she wouldn't scream out loud. Maybe it wouldn't find her. Maybe she could hide.

Then a dark figure, tall and spare, stepped from the trees. Elizabeth felt as if she were made of plaster: light, insubstantial, incapable of movement. Slowly the figure came closer and closer to her, and Elizabeth's body began to tremble.

Her eyes frozen open, she gazed with horror

into the man's face, but it was shrouded in shadow. Then the faintest wash of moonlight crossed his features, and bright-green eyes stared down into her own.

Elizabeth almost sobbed with relief as she collapsed into his arms. She knew him.

"Don't worry, darling," the soothing voice said. "You're all right now. Soon you'll never have to worry about being hurt again. Soon nothing will be able to touch you. But you have to come with me."

Elizabeth nodded, and the man bent her head back and kissed her neck with sharp, stinging little kisses. When she moaned, he covered her lips with his own, sweeping her into his arms and holding her tightly against him. Warmth flowed over Elizabeth as she clung to him, kissing him back deeply, her hands twined in his dark hair. "Don't leave me," she whispered, panting for breath.

"I'll never leave you," he promised. Again and again they kissed, their mouths parted as if their very life forces were joining in their breaths. Soon Elizabeth felt her head swimming, felt her gaze dim. She was floating deliciously, she was warm and safe, she had never been so blissful, so at ease. . . .

"You must come with me," he said, pulling himself out of her arms. He began to walk backward into the woods, beckoning her. Smiling, Elizabeth slowly followed him.

*   *   *

Tom's breath caught in his throat as his arms pumped by his sides. His sneakered feet pounded against the sidewalk but didn't make much noise. The night air was cool and refreshingly damp against his heated skin, and he felt his sweat trickle down his temples.

It was pretty pathetic to be jogging late at night by himself, he knew. But after rattling around his room alone for an hour, he'd felt as if he would explode with energy and frustration. If Danny had been there, they could have gone for a pizza or even just sat around and talked. But Danny was with his girlfriend, Isabella.

The toss of a coin had determined whether Tom would go running or take a long, icy shower. Running had won.

Actually, he thought it might be helping. With the blood pounding hard in his veins, his lungs feeling as if they were about to burst with each breath, he felt invigorated and renewed. When he had been a star football player, long endurance-building runs had been a regular part of his life. Since then he'd made it a point to keep in shape, and this run was no hardship for him.

To his right was a path that wound through the quad, past the student center and the library. To the left was a path that led to Dickenson Hall.

Watts, don't be a total wuss, he thought desperately. *Don't make me ashamed of you.* But he couldn't help himself. He veered to the left, cursing every pounding step. *What are you going to do? Stand under her dark window and howl? You are such a total loser.*

Another minute and he was almost upon the dorm. His steps slowed, his breathing deepened, and he gradually dropped to a walk. The sidewalk path was bordered on both sides by trees, and they hung over him, making him feel slightly less conspicuous. With a sudden, unexpected premonition, Tom whirled to look in back of him. He was alone. At this hour the campus was mostly silent and dark. He frowned. Then, ahead of him, about twenty yards away, he saw a movement.

A deeply black shadow had moved away from a tree for a minute, then blended back in. The quad spotlights highlighted the front of the dorm and spilled their orange halogen pools onto the grass. Then he saw the shadow again—the merest movement, the slightest gesture.

Tom stopped dead, his face flushing despite the quick rush of icy-cold air that washed over him. In the next moment he saw him. There was a figure standing beneath a tree in front of Dickenson Hall. Tom discerned a tall man, dressed all in black. And he was familiar to Tom—the way he stood, his height, his wiry body.

Tom's jaw dropped. Nicholas des Perdu was

here, in Sweet Valley. Tom blinked and started to move forward, then stopped again.

There was no man there—there was no one around except him. Now that he was closer, he could see the tree clearly, and it was bare and shadowy. Without pausing to think, Tom ran to the tree, and once around the trunk. But no one was there.

Could he have imagined the shadow? His eyes searched the whole area around the dorm, but he saw nothing. He must be hallucinating. Sighing, Tom wiped the sweat from his forehead and pushed his damp hair back. He was losing his mind. Not only was he stalking Elizabeth's dorm late at night, but he was imagining other people stalking her, too. And not just any other people. He was imagining a man whom he had met only once in his life, whom he knew to live more than two thousand miles away. It was ludicrous, absurd. He really felt pathetic.

I might as well wallow in self-pity, he thought in disgust. *Might as well totally humiliate myself.* Tom raised his eyes to Elizabeth's window. Although there was a light on, the shade was pulled up, the window open. Elizabeth, in a long nightgown, was standing right in front of the open window.

Tom stared up at her. Her eyes were open but appeared unseeing. Her arms were outstretched, though there was nothing there. Her skin was bloodless, leeched of color by the moonlight. What was she doing?

As he watched, his mouth hanging open, Elizabeth moved even closer to the open window. Unbelievably, she smiled into nothingness and actually leaned out the window.

Her lips parted, and soft words floated down to Tom. "I'm coming," he thought he heard her say. "I'm coming."

"Elizabeth!" he shouted in terror as she swayed even farther out the open window. "Elizabeth, stop it! Be careful!" Then, without waiting to see if she had responded to his voice, he rushed up the dorm steps and yanked the door open.

Chapter
Sixteen

Once inside Dickenson Hall, Tom took the stairs two at a time. It seemed like hours before he reached Elizabeth's floor, and then he was racing down the hall.

"Elizabeth!" he yelled again, praying he wasn't too late. He reached the door, banging on it. When he tried to turn the doorknob, he realized it was locked. "Elizabeth!"

Several rooms down, the RA's door opened and she stepped out, looking angry. "What do you think you're doing?" she demanded. "Do you know what time it is?"

"Open this door!" Tom yelled, slamming his open fist against it. "Something's wrong!"

By this time other doors were opening along the hall, and bleary-eyed students peered out to see what was happening.

"Don't tell me it's another fire," someone complained sleepily.

"Open this door!" Tom shouted again.

The RA came toward him with her passkey. Looking doubtfully at Tom, she knocked loudly on Elizabeth's door.

"Elizabeth? It's Caryn. Let me in."

"Open it!"

Caryn opened the door and Tom burst through. To his horror Elizabeth was tilting slowly, out the window. The night wind was blowing her hair and her long nightgown back; the moonlight was outlining her cheek and the side of her neck.

"Liz!" Tom shouted, leaping toward her. Just as Elizabeth seemed ready to topple forward, he grabbed her shoulders, yanking her back roughly. He pulled her easily into the room as Caryn and a few others crowded in.

Elizabeth lay quietly in Tom's arms, her eyes closed, her breathing shallow and light.

"Close that window," he snapped. Caryn bustled to close it and latch it shut.

"What's going on?" Caryn asked. "Is she OK?"

Tom smoothed Elizabeth's hair back and gently patted her cheek. "Elizabeth. Elizabeth, wake up." He realized with surprise that his voice was shaking and his knees felt weak. Still holding Elizabeth, he sank down onto her bed and pulled her into his lap.

"Come on, Elizabeth, wake up."

Caryn shooed the other students out of the room and shut the door. Then she came back to Tom with a wet washcloth.

"Should I call an ambulance?" she asked quietly. "Do you think she's been doing drugs?"

Tom looked up in shock. "No! Elizabeth would never do that."

"Tom?" Elizabeth's hand fluttered up to the wet cloth on her forehead. Her eyes looked sleepy, her pupils large and dark. She picked up the cloth and looked at it in bemusement. Tom helped her sit up. "What are you doing here?"

"I . . . was just walking by," he said awkwardly. "And I saw you—"

"What's going on?" Elizabeth asked, looking from Tom to Caryn.

"That's what I want to know," Caryn said, folding her arms across the nightgown she had worn to bed. "You were about to jump out your window."

"What?" Elizabeth's eyes popped open, and she sat up straighter. "What do you mean?"

"When we came in, you were sort of . . . falling out your window," Tom explained.

"That's impossible!" Elizabeth exclaimed. She rubbed her fist across her eyes and looked at her window.

"We shut it," Caryn said. "Now, Elizabeth,

200

what's going on? Are you upset about something? Have you been down lately?"

Elizabeth stared at the RA in horror. "No! I wasn't going to jump! I don't know what you're talking about. I was asleep. . . ."

A confused expression crossed her face, and she pushed her hair behind her shoulders. "I was sleeping," she repeated, her brows creasing in a frown. "I was having a bad dream. . . ."

"Maybe you were sleepwalking," Tom suggested uncertainly.

"Me? No . . ." Elizabeth frowned off into the distance.

"Look, what are we going to do here?" Caryn asked briskly. "Is Jessica due back soon?"

"No." Elizabeth shook her head, still looking confused, and, Tom thought, almost a little scared. "She's staying over at the Theta house."

"I could stay here," Tom offered. "On Jessica's bed." The three of them looked doubtfully at Jessica's nestlike bed, with its bundled, undone covers and thick layer of clothes, books, magazines, and CDs.

"Oh, no, that's OK," Elizabeth said. "You don't have to do that. I don't know what happened, but I'm sure I'll be fine now."

Caryn shook her head. "I think Tom's right. If Jessica isn't coming back, I think one of us should stay here with you. Then tomorrow, if you still feel weird, you can go to the clinic and get checked out."

"Maybe Caryn should stay with you," Tom said stiffly. He hoped that Elizabeth would say she wanted *him* to stay, but he wasn't going to force her into anything. Not the way she had been acting lately.

"I really don't mind," Caryn said firmly.

"I guess," Elizabeth said slowly, looking down at the floor. "If you're sure."

Tom's heart sank to his feet, but he tried not to let his disappointment show. She had been rejecting him at every turn, and he had no idea why. But right now wasn't the time or the place to pursue the matter. He stood up.

"OK. I'll feel better, knowing you're here," he told Caryn.

Bending down, he kissed Elizabeth's forehead but didn't meet her eyes. "I'll see you tomorrow morning," he reminded her. "When we go decorate the old Hollow House."

Elizabeth nodded, still looking at the floor. When Tom closed the door behind him, he felt overcome with hopelessness.

"Hash browns?" the cafeteria worker asked Jessica.

Jessica looked down at them, savoring their aroma.

"Please." She couldn't watch what she ate *all* the time. After collecting two cups of coffee, she went through the checkout and found herself a spot at an empty table.

Breakfast was almost over—she had made it just in time. She could have used a couple more hours sleep. After she ate, she would run back to her dorm room and repair the damage to her looks that her sleepless night had caused.

"Jessica—hi."

Without turning around Jessica heaved a mental sigh. She took a bite of hash browns and then put down her fork.

"Hi, Tom," she said unenthusiastically as he sat down across from her. "Don't tell me—let me guess. You're looking for Elizabeth."

Tom's face flushed, and Jessica felt a stab of pity. He really was too easy a target.

"No, it's not that," he said, his voice tight. "I was just wondering if *you've* seen her this morning. Did she tell you about what happened last night?"

Jessica took a big swig of hot coffee. "No and no," she answered. "What happened last night? I mean, besides the fact that I brought my sleeping bag to sleep in my new room, and much to my horror Alison Quinn *also* brought her sleeping bag and slept in my new room, and we were there together glaring at each other all night?"

"Elizabeth was sleepwalking," Tom said tersely.

Eyebrows raised, Jessica said, "Really? You're kidding. That's really interesting. I've never known anyone who sleepwalked before. Is it *sleep*walked or *slept*walked? What do you think?" She buttered her toast briskly.

"I think you won't think it's so funny when you hear that your twin almost jumped out your dorm window. Caryn Perini and I both saw her. In fact, after that Caryn stayed in your room all night, to keep an eye on Elizabeth."

Jessica's blue-green eyes, identical to Elizabeth's, stared at Tom. "Whaaaat?"

Quickly Tom explained everything he had seen the night before.

"Jeez," Jessica said when he was finished. "That girl is coming unglued."

"Do you really think so?" Tom asked seriously. "I mean, should we intervene?"

After thinking about it for a minute, Jessica shook her head slowly. "I don't really think so," she said. "Maybe she's just feeling kind of stressed. Maybe she's coming down with something, like the flu. I tell you what—we'll all be decorating that creepy old mansion for the party tonight. Let's each keep our eyes on her, and we'll talk again if she does anything strange. But if she seems more or less normal, we won't worry about it. OK?"

Indecision crossed Tom's face, but finally he nodded. "OK. Are you going back to the dorm?

Tell Elizabeth I'll be by to take her to the old Hollow House in about twenty minutes."

"Sure thing," Jessica said.

"Tape this end up there." Jessica pointed to a wall and held up one end of her crepe-paper streamer.

"All right." Elizabeth, on a ladder, took the end and stretched it to the dining-room wall. The twisted strands of orange and black fluttered into place as she taped them down securely. "That looks great," she said, smiling down at Jessica. "Let's do a couple more, and then this room will be finished."

"I feel like I've been here for *days*," Jessica said, examining the grit under her fingernails. "What time is it?"

"Two thirty." Elizabeth grinned. "You've been here forty-five minutes."

"Stop it, Winnie! Stop it!" Denise Waters ran through the dining room shrieking as Winston Egbert chased after her, spraying her with a can of artificial spiderwebs. They disappeared into the sunroom, though Denise's cries could still be heard.

Elizabeth looked around in satisfaction. They would be done in another hour—plenty of time before the party, which didn't start until nine. Despite her feelings of confusion about her romantic life, she had actually managed to get this party organized.

"Where's the boy wonder?" Jessica asked, twisting together another strand of orange-and-black crepe paper.

"I assume you mean Tom," Elizabeth said dryly. "He's in the ballroom, getting things ready for the band."

"He told me about what happened last night," Jessica said with studied casualness, handing her streamer up to Elizabeth.

Elizabeth made a face. "I bet he made it sound worse than it was," she said. "It really wasn't a big deal. I've just been really stressed lately. But now that this party will be off my shoulders, I can take it a little easier. I think I might go home next weekend, for some rest and TLC."

"That sounds good," Jessica said, brushing her hands off on her jeans. "A couple days of professional mothering, and you'll feel like a new woman."

"Exactly." Elizabeth climbed down from the ladder and consulted her list. "But I *am* really excited about this party. I've been looking forward to it for ages, and it's going to be great. Probably everyone will be talking about it for years to come."

I wish Nicholas could come. Quickly she banished the thought from her head. She'd tried to think of a rational way to explain his presence at the party, if she invited him, but couldn't really come up with anything convincing. Also, if he came, the night would probably turn into a huge disaster: For some strange reason she felt powerless when she was around him, as if she wore her emotions written all over her face. She didn't want to risk doing that in front of Tom. Not until she figured out what was going on, what she was going to do.

Elizabeth tapped her clipboard. "OK, all we have left in here is to set up the tables with the paper tablecloths."

She and Jessica started unfolding the rented tables. There was a large bag with paper goods in it, and they dug out the tablecloths.

"So you're not the only one who had some excitement last night," Jessica said, taping one tablecloth into place. "Apparently Alison had the exact same idea that I had and showed up with *her* sleeping bag."

"Oh, no," Elizabeth laughed. "What did you do?"

"She's such a copycat," Jessica complained. "She absolutely refused to leave, so what could I do? We both lay there in the dark, listening to each other breathe. I was scared to go to sleep— she probably would have painted little hearts and flowers all over the walls if I had. I'm going to have to take a nap later if I want to stay up late tonight." Her eyes twinkled at Elizabeth. "And I *do* want to stay up late tonight. Randy hasn't seen my costume yet, but when he does . . ."

Elizabeth shook her head as they set up another table. "You and Randy Mason," she marveled. "*Anyone* and Randy Mason. The mind boggles."

"He's fabulous. But I know what you mean. It's like Lila and Bruce Patman."

"Uh-huh."

"Speaking of costumes, what are you and Tom going to wear?"

Elizabeth sighed. "We never really did decide," she said. "I'm not sure what he's going as, but I'm sort of stuck with recycling my old witch costume from last year."

"You guys are going together, aren't you?"

"I guess so." Elizabeth sighed again. "We haven't really talked about it. OK, we're almost done," she said, stepping back to admire their work. "I think the place looks great. We can take it from here, Jessica, if you want to go home and nap for a while. Or maybe you need to go back to Theta house and stake your claim for a couple hours."

"Laugh if you must," Jessica said haughtily. "But that room will be mine. And it'll be fabulous. But, actually, I don't think I need to worry about Alison taking it over—at least not today." Her face was innocent and unconcerned.

"Uh-oh," Elizabeth said suspiciously. "I know that face. What have you done?"

Jessica beamed at her triumphantly. "This

morning after she left, I hired a locksmith to come out. He put a new padlock on the door, and only *I* have the key." She laughed at her own sneakiness.

"Oh," Elizabeth moaned. "You're going to be the death of that girl."

"With any luck at all," Jessica confirmed happily.

" 'Vampire' Killer Strikes Again."

Tom's gaze was riveted by the headline of the local newspaper. With an odd feeling of dread he pushed his coffee cup aside and began to read the story. The late-afternoon sun streamed in through the window of the Coffee House and fell across the newspaper. Tom shielded the story with his hand.

According to the police report, another blood-drained victim had been found early that morning at the very edge of the SVU campus. Caroline Simpson, an assistant teacher at SVU, had been found beside her car. Although her car door had been open, there had been no sign of a robbery or struggle. The victim had been found sitting on the grass, leaning against her car, every bit of blood drained from her body. The police were assuming that it was the work of the same killer who had already struck twice, and cautioned people to be especially careful as they celebrated Halloween that night.

After Tom read the story, he sat at his table, staring off into the distance. This was just too weird.

First there had been the deaths in New Orleans. Now the exact same kind of killer was loose at Sweet Valley University. On top of everything, Elizabeth was acting really weird, and Tom himself was imagining things. Things like seeing Nicholas des Perdu staring up at Elizabeth's window.

"I'm going crazy," Tom muttered, draining the last of his coffee. Then he grabbed the newspaper, threw some money onto the table, and raced out of the Coffee House.

Chapter Seventeen

As a reporter and a journalism major, Tom was well-known at the local newspaper morgue. The small, dusty room in the basement of the main newspaper offices was filled with microfiche machines and file cabinets. He had spent endless hours there, researching his stories, getting background information, and tracking down sources.

Now he dumped his backpack onto a table and flipped on the light of one of the microfiche machines. Then he searched the "recent" files for the latest films of *The New Orleans Times-Picayune*. He started with newspapers from two days before he had arrived in New Orleans and went through every single day until Wednesday, which was the most recent day they had.

In New Orleans, before Tom had arrived and until the day after he had left, there had been a rash of unexplained "vampire killings," where the victim was found drained of blood after no visible struggle. Breathing fast, Tom made notes. The victims were all below the age of forty, and most of them were in their twenties. There were more females than males. Most of the deaths took place either in or near the French Quarter. Other than that, there was no pattern.

The deaths had stopped on Monday.

Next Tom pulled the films for the local paper, starting with last Friday and continuing through yesterday. The first local deaths had occurred on Tuesday night. The victim profiles were the same as those from New Orleans—that is, no real pattern except they were young and healthy.

"OK, OK," Tom muttered. "What does this mean?" He sat back in his chair and stared at his notes.

Ten minutes later he snapped his pencil in half. It all meant exactly nothing. The only way he would have any kind of story is if he could link the deaths to one person.

Finally he had to ask himself the hundred-thousand-dollar question: What did he suspect? Was he thinking that Nicholas des Perdu had something to do with the deaths? Oh, *that* made a lot of sense. Just because the man lived in a city where a killer was on the loose, and because Tom *thought* he *might* have seen him here, in another city, where the same killer was apparently operating . . . It still added up to nothing.

Basically, Tom's imagination, his frustration and worry about Elizabeth, and his overinquisitive reporter's mind was suggesting that one of the world's top journalists, a man who had been famous for years, was, in fact, a serial killer with a weird vampire obsession.

A man who had been famous for years.

How old was Nicholas des Perdu, anyway? When Tom had tried to research him briefly, before going to New Orleans, he hadn't been able to find very much information at all. No one seemed to know his birthplace, his education history, his age . . . But Tom knew he had been famous for years. And yet he looked so young.

Which means . . . what?

Nothing.

OK, Watts. Let's see you do some actual investigative reporting. Let's find out one fact. Is Nicholas des Perdu even in the Sweet Valley area?

Tom picked up his backpack and went outside to his car.

"Is Randy picking you up for the party?" Elizabeth asked as she and Jessica returned to their dorm after dinner on Friday night.

Jessica shook her head. "Uh-uh. I'm meeting him there. I have to stop by the Theta house first."

"Well, I haven't talked to Tom since this morning—I guess we're going together, but we didn't make it definite," Elizabeth said, pulling her room key out of her pocket.

"You could call him now," Jessica pointed out.

Elizabeth nodded unenthusiastically and unlocked their door.

The room was dark inside, and the first thing she was aware of was the heavy scent of roses billowing out to meet them.

Elizabeth stepped into the room and flicked on the light switch.

"Oh, my gosh," she said.

"Wow, are they from Randy?" Jessica squealed, pushing past Elizabeth into the room and starting to search for a card. Their small dorm room was packed with masses of roses—huge glass vases of dozens and dozens of long-stemmed white roses. Their heavy scent, released into the warm air of the room, swirled around Elizabeth until she felt almost dizzy.

No. They're not from Randy, Elizabeth thought, feeling that she knew instantly what the card would say, if there was a card. Her stomach tightened, her fingers clenched by her sides. A breathless feeling of anticipation raced through her, making her feel excited and tingly all over.

"Here!" Jessica found one bouquet on Elizabeth's desk with a card attached. Alone of all the bouquets, this one had a single blood-red rose right in the middle of the white ones. Jessica pounced on the card and ripped it open.

After reading it eagerly, she frowned. "I don't get it." She tossed the card to Elizabeth.

Slowly Elizabeth took the card. Her hand was practically trembling, her palm damp with sweat. Maybe he missed her as much as she missed him.

We'll be together tonight. N.

Yes, he did miss her.

"Who's N?" Jessica demanded, burying her face in some of the flowers and breathing deeply. "Do you think it's a mistake?" She looked up in horror. "Maybe these were all for someone else. Maybe we should . . . give them back."

Elizabeth knew that even if they *had* been for someone else, Jessica would rather have all her fingernails pulled out with pliers than give them back.

She smiled at her sister. "I don't know who they're from," she said, feeling amazingly calm at lying to Jessica. "But they're gorgeous. I'm sure they're meant for one of us—let's just wait and see. Maybe N is a secret admirer." Her breath was coming fast and shallow, but Jessica didn't seem to notice.

"OK," Jessica acquiesced immediately. "Hmm, they're absolutely heavenly." She glanced at her watch. "Great. It's past seven. I better run over to the Theta house and check on my stuff. Then I'll come back here and get ready. You'll be here, right?"

Elizabeth nodded, trying to seem natural. "Yeah. I'm just going to rest for a while and then get ready for the party."

"OK. Just don't go sleepwalking or anything," Jessica said with a grin.

"OK." Elizabeth grinned back. Then Jessica whirled out of the room, slamming the door behind her in typical Jessica fashion.

After she was gone, Elizabeth walked around the room slowly, gently touching each rose of each bouquet, letting their sweet, exotic scent wash over her. Breathing in their fragrance was like drinking wine, she thought. It was making her feel dizzy and reckless, giddy and full of a daring power.

She had never seen so many roses in her life, so many perfect, icy-white roses.

All of yesterday and today she had been trying hard not to think about Nicholas, not to think about the way she had felt in his arms. But it now seemed inevitable that they would be together. She'd been fighting her feelings, because despite her overwhelming pull toward Nicholas, she knew she still loved Tom. But it was beyond her control.

Now she realized that Nicholas was always on her mind, that the memory of his kisses, his jade eyes, the touch of his strong, cool fingers, was always with her. She should just give in. She couldn't ignore her destiny any longer. She didn't want to.

Gently she stroked her finger along the petals of the one red rose. The flower was so dark and soft and velvety, she felt like she was touching blood.

"Ow," Elizabeth said under her breath, pulling back her hand. A sharp thorn had punctured the skin of her thumb, and she gazed in fascination at the dark, fat drop of blood that oozed out. She put her thumb in her mouth and sucked on it, tasting the metallic, salty tang.

When the phone rang, she wasn't surprised.

"Hello?"

"My dear, yesterday was desolate without you," came the smooth, familiar tones that made her head swim. At the sound of his voice, the room seemed suddenly small and too warm and too full of the scent of roses.

"I know," Elizabeth whispered, sitting on her bed.

"We'll be together tonight, yes?"

Something inside Elizabeth, some last vestige of free will, shrank and died at the question. Suddenly she felt like a kite whose string had snapped, leaving her free to float into the atmosphere on a strong current.

"Yes," Elizabeth said softly, lying down. She curled up on her side, cradling the phone against

217

one ear. "I have to go to the Monster Madness benefit party," she added. "At least for a while."

"All right," he said understandingly. "But I will pick you up at the end of the road leading to the old Hollow House, at midnight. You'll be ready?"

"Yes," Elizabeth said again. She felt as if she were speaking through a fog, as if the phone were very far away and it was hard to make herself heard.

"Good. Tonight, my darling, we'll be together. And I will take you to my home. Then we'll never be parted again. Not for all eternity."

His voice was like rose petals brushing against her cheek. Suddenly Elizabeth was filled with an overwhelming desire to see him, to hold him, to be one with him.

"I'll see you at midnight," she promised.

"À bientôt."

When Elizabeth hung up the phone, she felt drained but excited. Glancing at the clock, she saw it was almost eight. She really should start getting ready for the party.

In front of the Sweet Valley Grande Hotel, Tom braced himself and threw back his shoulders. In the last three hours he had gone to seven different hotels, trying to find evidence of Nicholas des Perdu being in town. The Grande was his last hope.

This whole thing is stupid, anyway, he told himself. *I must be going crazy.*

218

And yet Tom knew that he couldn't just give up without trying everything that came to mind. There was a bigger picture somewhere, he knew. All he had was some of the edge pieces, but he knew if he could just find the overall pattern, everything would fall into place.

In the meantime I'm chasing a feather down a street, he thought bitterly. Well, this was it—his last stop. A few minutes ago he had tried to call Elizabeth to tell her he would be late getting back to campus. But her line had been busy—Jessica was probably yakking up a storm. He would try again in a few minutes.

Resolutely he pushed through the brass revolving doors of the Grande. A clerk, looking barely older than Tom, smiled as he approached the reservations desk.

"Good evening. May I help you, sir?" the clerk asked with professional formality.

"Yes." Tom gave the clerk what he thought of as his "innocent" smile. "My uncle left me a message saying that he's in town and staying here. His name is Nicholas des Perdu. Could you just tell me his room number, please?" Tom gave another toothy smile. *Come on, come on, come on.*

The clerk looked uncomfortable. "Uh, I'm sorry, sir. But guests of the Grande value their privacy. They come here precisely because they know we'll do our utmost to be discreet."

Tom gave the clerk the same disbelieving look he had given seven other clerks. "But he's my uncle!" he cried. "He left a message for me to meet him here."

The clerk looked unhappy, but firm. "I'm really sorry, sir. I understand your frustration. If you'd like to leave a message for your uncle, I could see that he gets it, *if* he's a guest at this hotel. But I can't verify that or give you his room number. It's hotel policy."

For a moment Tom wanted to grab the clerk by the lapels and haul him over the counter, the way he had seen people do in movies. Fortunately, he realized that he didn't have a movie star's impunity.

So what should he do? Admit defeat? Slink back to his dorm room with his tail between his legs?

Suddenly another customer came up to the counter, and the clerk, with a final apologetic glance at Tom, moved over to wait on him.

Leaning against the counter despondently, Tom decided he should go back to his dorm and call Elizabeth. It was almost eight o'clock, and she would have to leave for the party soon. He still needed to get into his recycled pirate costume. Then his eye fell on a sheaf of papers on the other side of the counter. It was the computerized check-in list for October 31. Today. Tom glanced at the clerk. There was apparently a problem with the person's bill, and the clerk was anxiously trying to straighten the matter out. Neither the clerk nor the customer seemed the slightest bit aware of Tom.

Looking around surreptitiously, Tom saw that no one seemed to be paying attention to him whatsoever. He didn't think twice but shot his hand over the counter, ripped off the top page, and stuffed it into his pocket. Three seconds later the other customer went away, and the clerk came back, looking frazzled.

"Well, maybe I should just go home and wait for Uncle Nicholas to call again." Tom tried to sound meek.

"Perhaps that would be best," the clerk agreed with obvious relief.

"Thanks, anyway," Tom said graciously as he turned to leave.

"Our pleasure, sir."

"I do *not* believe this," Jessica ground out through clenched teeth. Her face flushed with anger, she stared at the new padlock that she'd had the locksmith place on her Theta-room door. It had been neatly hacksawed through the hasp and was hanging morosely from its fitting. On the door itself a brand-new, shiny dead-bolt lock seemed to mock her.

Her jaw clenched, Jessica reached out and gave the knob a vicious twist. It turned uselessly in her hand.

"Jessica? Is that you?" came the muffled, triumphant voice from within the room.

Jessica's eyes flew open in rage. *Alison!* She was actually *in* the room right at this very minute! While Jessica stood like a beggar outside. It was unendurable!

"Open the door this minute!" Jessica hissed, whacking the door hard with her hand. "Or else!"

Inside, Alison laughed infuriatingly. "Or else what? You'll huff and you'll puff and you'll blow the house down? I have to say, if anyone has enough hot air, it would be you."

Jessica couldn't remember the last time she'd been so angry. If Alison had been right there, Jessica thought she might have slapped her.

"You know that room is mine!" Jessica cried. "When are you going to get that through your thick skull?"

"Excuse me?" Alison said, laughing. "Could you speak up, Jessica? My thick skull is having a hard time hearing you."

"Oooh! Ow ow ow!" Jessica kicked the door as hard as she could but succeeded only in possibly fracturing her pinkie toe. For a couple of minutes she hopped around, gritting her teeth silently through pain. She rubbed her foot and cursed Alison Quinn beneath her breath.

After a few minutes Alison called through the door. "Jessica? Are you still there?"

"Who wants to know?" Jessica snarled, leaning against the wall, trying desperately to come up with some kind of plan.

"Know what I'm doing?" Alison taunted.

"Why would I care?"

"I'm sitting at my lace-covered makeup table, getting ready for tonight's Monster Madness party. I have everything I need right in here with me. And when I'm ready to leave, I'm going to lock the door behind me."

I hate this girl, Jessica seethed. *I hate her more than anyone I've ever known in my entire life.*

"Drop dead," Jessica snapped, then turned and stomped loudly down the hall. It was hard to stomp with one possibly fractured toe, but Jessica did her best.

The intensely irritating sound of Alison's high-pitched laughter followed her.

It's not that easy to get the better of Jessica Wakefield, Jessica thought moments later, as she entered the Theta house's side yard through the wooden gate. Her new room looked out over the yard. Maybe she could intimidate Alison through the window. Maybe she could even climb in somehow, although what she would do after that wasn't clear. Have a screaming catfight? Punch Alison in the nose? She could just hear Magda Helperin's elegant, modulated voice saying that she didn't think Jessica's actions represented desirable Theta behavior.

As she rounded the corner of the house, Jessica shivered. The beautiful fall day was turning into a nasty fall night. Although the moon was full, it was mostly obscured by a thick covering of heavy rain clouds. The wind had picked up, and the temperature had dropped. It looked as if it would rain at any second. Now Jessica could see the filtered yellow light from the open window of her new room. It was shining through Alison's revolting lace curtains, and the knowledge made her grit her teeth.

Just as Alison came to the window to pull it shut, Jessica saw a dark shadow detach itself from the clump of palm trees that stood next to the fence.

Instinctively, Jessica ducked back against a corner of the house, out of sight. So! Goody-two-shoes Alison Quinn was meeting strange guys through her window! Jessica frowned, wondering why she didn't just let him in the front door. It wasn't forbidden to have male visitors at Theta house. A sneer curled her lip. Alison probably thought it was more romantic to have her date come to the window. Like Romeo or something.

A chill wind blew through the yard and rustled Jessica's hair. She wrapped her arms around herself. Sighing, she decided to go meet Elizabeth back at their room. She'd have to deal with Alison later.

As she turned to leave the yard, she heard a

beautiful, cultured male voice say, "Hello."

There was a pause, and as Jessica let herself out through the gate again, she heard Alison's response. "Well. Hello there."

Oh, please, Jessica thought derisively. *Gag me with a spoon.*

Chapter
Eighteen

Tom let the phone ring about twelve times, mentally willing Elizabeth to be in her room. Just as he was about to hang up, he heard the click of the receiver.

"Hello?"

It had taken Tom a couple of weeks, when he and Elizabeth had first started dating, to distinguish her voice from Jessica's. His ears still burned when he remembered some of the private and romantic things Jessica had let him say, thinking she was Elizabeth. Since then, of course, the two girls had become as distinct as vanilla and chocolate.

"Elizabeth?" It was definitely Elizabeth, but she didn't sound like herself.

"Oh. Tom."

Jeez. Maybe you could be even less enthusiastic.

"Yeah—I'm sorry I didn't call before. I've been . . . working on a story."

"That's OK. Jessica and I were already out the door to go to the party. We came back because I forgot my key. I figured I would just see you there."

"I could be ready in just a second, if you'd rather wait for me to run over."

"No, that's OK," Elizabeth's cool voice continued. "We really should get to the party a little early, since we're the hosts. Take your time, and I'll see you there."

Tom frowned at the phone. Maybe she really *was* trying to dump him. Her voice sounded so distant, so uncaring, that he felt as if he were talking to a recording. "Yeah, sure," he muttered. "I'll see you in a little while. And, Elizabeth?"

"Yeah?"

"Please be careful tonight," he said gruffly. "Don't go anywhere by yourself, and just—be careful."

"See you later, Tom."

After he hung up, Tom cradled the phone against his chest for a minute. If only he knew what was going on with her. One of his favorite things about Elizabeth was that she was always really straightforward about her feelings. She didn't play mind games. It was always just right there, out in the open. But lately she had been avoiding him, had been denying that anything was wrong. She'd been distant and cool—it was enough to make him go crazy.

Think about something else. It wasn't even nine o'clock yet, so Tom had a little while before he absolutely had to get to the party.

Pulling out the crumpled guest register from the Sweet Valley Grande, Tom spread it on his desk and began to go down the list of names.

"Jessica!" Isabella Ricci yelled over the blare of the Teenage Zombies. "Amazing party!" She made a thumbs-up gesture, almost spilling her glass of punch.

"Thanks!" Jessica yelled back, twirling her Catwoman tail with one hand. It was true. The party was a huge success. The Hollow House was packed with writhing costumed bodies. The band was great, and the music was actually rattling the windows and the chandeliers. The atmosphere was totally creepy, yet festive. Outside, the wind was picking up, and leaves were swirling against the grimy windows. But inside there were hundreds of black-and-orange candles giving a warm glow to the rooms, and the combination of dancing bodies and potent "Blood Punch" had warmed the air considerably.

In front of Jessica, a guy in full costume, who Jessica thought might be a Zeta brother, stopped and leaned toward her. He had an orange pump-kin-shaped cookie in his mouth and gestured that she should bite the other half.

Jessica giggled and looked around quickly for Randy, who was dressed as a mad scientist. There he was, dancing with Nina Harper. Tilting her head up, Jessica let her eyes twinkle at the guy, then took a careful bite of the cookie. They grinned at each other; then the guy moved on to the sunporch to get another drink.

Fortunately, she hadn't seen Alison yet. There was no concrete plan so far, but Jessica was sure that she could manage to lift the punch bowl by herself and fling it onto her beloved Theta sister. She would have to play it by ear.

Moments later Elizabeth drifted by in her witch costume. She had taken the one red rose from the bouquet and pinned it to her cape. Jessica grabbed her arm, and Elizabeth looked up in surprise.

"This is so great!" Jessica yelled. "Can we throw a party, or can we throw a party?"

Elizabeth smiled and nodded. "We've raised a lot of money for the women's shelter, and more people keep coming all the time. I hope the food holds out."

Jessica shrugged. "In another hour no one will notice if there's any food left or not. Have you seen Lila's costume?"

"It's incredible," Elizabeth acknowledged. "She really looks like Elvira."

"I've never seen Bruce stare at anything with such fascination," Jessica said snidely. "Except, of course, a *mirror*."

Elizabeth laughed softly. "I haven't seen a few people yet—like Denise, or Tom."

"They'll be here," Jessica said with an airy wave of her hand. "The night is young."

Through the window Elizabeth could look up and see the soft yellow fullness of the full moon. "Yes," she said. "The night is young."

Leaning out the window, Nicholas looked up at the sky. Dark, heavy clouds were blowing across the full moon's surface, blocking its light, then revealing it in all its glory.

Behind him he heard a knock on the door. "Alison? It's Magda and Denise," a female voice said. "Come on, we're late for the party. Are you ready?"

Nighttime was a beautiful time, Nicholas thought, easing himself through the window frame and landing easily and silently on the soft ground below. The night was so much more compelling than the day. Night was subtle, day was obvious. Night was silken, day was harsh. Night was welcoming, cool, seductive. Day was glaring, burning, hostile.

"Alison?" The knocks increased in strength, the voice got louder. Nicholas faded into the cluster of palm trees in the side yard.

"Alison? Come on, open up." The door rattled.

Nicholas heard a second voice say, "Did she give you a key to the new lock?"

"Yes," the first voice answered. "It's a house rule. Maybe she fell asleep or something."

An unamused smile shifted the planes of Nicholas's face as he slipped through the trees toward the side gate. He had to get everything ready. Midnight would arrive soon, though it still felt years away.

Inside the house he had just left, a key turned in a lock; a door opened.

Then two female voices, raised in terrified screams, pierced the night.

Forty-five people had checked into the Grande between two and six P.M. None of them was named Nicholas des Perdu.

"Shoot!" Tom rocked back in his desk chair and ran his hands through his hair, making it stand up. *Think, Watts, think. What's going on here?*

He took a deep breath and looked at the list again. There were seven people with the first initial *N*. It was impossible to tell if they were male or female or what the *N* stood for. In desperation Tom reread their last names.

N. Marcosi. N. Thompson. N. Varela. N. Ofthelost. N. Milford. N. Fory. N. Nicholson.

"Nicholson?" Nicholas Nicholson. Would he have really done that? Tom refused to admit to himself how tenuous the connection was. But he couldn't see any other clue at all. None of the other names meant anything at all . . . *Ofthelost*. What kind of weird name was that? It sounded Swedish or something. Then, as Tom stared at the black letters marching like ants across the page, the name seemed to separate into little groups. Ofthelost. Of the lost. *Of The Lost*.

"Hmm." Tom pinched his lip between his thumb and forefinger, the way he did when he was thinking hard. OK. Given this humongous stretch of likelihood, what did that mean? Nicholas des Perdu. Des Perdu was French, obviously—did it mean something? Or was it just a place name, like Chambord? Tom got up and went over to his roommate's bookshelf. He grabbed Danny's French-English dictionary. *Here we go*.

Flipping through the pages to the P's, Tom found *perdu* without any trouble.

"*Perdu* (adj.): lost; ruined; spoilt; stray."

Oh, my God.

Nicholas des Perdu. N. Ofthelost.

He's in town.

It was the missing piece of the puzzle. Tom

jumped up and began to throw on his pirate's costume.

"Wow," Jessica purred, taking a sip of punch. She and Lila were standing by the refreshment table, trying to catch their breath. It was almost midnight, and they had both been dancing to almost every song. Soon it would be time for the costume contest, and the announcement of the final total for the evening's take.

"What?" Lila asked, flinging her long Elvira wig back over her shoulder. She raised a cold can of diet soda to her forehead and rolled it over her damp brow.

"*Who* is *that*?" Jessica gestured at a guy standing on the other side of the room. He was tall, though not as tall as Randy, and had dark-blond slightly wavy hair and a great tan.

"Ah," Lila said smugly. "You mean Louis Miles? Yes, he *is* cute, isn't he?"

"Is he in one of your classes?" Jessica asked with interest.

"You might say that," Lila answered, watching Jessica's face.

"He is what I call gorgeous." Jessica clasped her hands together.

Lila laughed. "Down, girl."

"Yo, Tom."

A guy from Tom's history class greeted

him, waving a plastic cup of blood-red punch at him. Tom nodded at him, noting that the Monster Madness party was going strong. It was almost midnight, and people were gearing themselves up for the costume contest. He looked around for Elizabeth but didn't see her. Slowly, he began to push his way through the crowd.

On his way over to the party, he'd had a flashback to his time in New Orleans. He'd remembered how Nicholas had stared so strangely at Elizabeth's photograph. He'd remembered how the picture had disappeared one night, then reappeared with a tiny stain on it. And for the first time he'd realized what he had seen in Nicholas's basement in New Orleans—what had imprinted itself onto his mind right before Marielle had found him on the basement stairs. Nicholas had had a coffin in his basement.

Now Nicholas was in town, possibly hanging out in front of Elizabeth's window, and Elizabeth was acting bizarrely. There had to be a connection.

Where was she?

It was impossible to move through the rooms quickly, but Tom was big, and as an ex-football player, he had experience getting through crowds. He went through all the rooms downstairs, even opening the hall closet, where he found a surprised couple. He found nothing upstairs either, although he hovered outside the women's bathroom for a while.

With a sense of growing panic, he realized he would have to rely on Jessica yet again. It was getting totally embarrassing, how often he asked her about Elizabeth. But he had no choice.

He found Jessica hovering in the middle of a group of girls, probably Thetas. They were all talking and giggling at the top of their lungs.

For once Jessica didn't sigh impatiently when she saw Tom approaching.

"Tom!" she shrieked. "Hi! Having a good time?"

"Yeah." Tom nodded. "Listen, have you—"

"Seen Elizabeth?" several of the girls chorused, then giggled again, exchanging glances.

Tom flushed in embarrassment. "Can I talk to you in private?" he asked Jessica, taking her arm.

Buoyed up by the success of the party, still laughing and joking with her friends, Jessica allowed him to lead her through the kitchen and out onto the dark, rickety back porch. Once there, she suddenly seemed to realize that they had left the party, and her face lost some of its happy excitement.

"Tom, what is this?" she complained, rubbing her arms with her hands. "It's freezing out here."

Until that moment Tom had had no idea of what he would say, what argument he would use to enlist Jessica's help. Now, terrified at the thought of Elizabeth's possibly being in the clutches of a killer, Tom awkwardly blurted out his suspicions.

"Jessica, do you remember my internship in New Orleans?"

"What? Oh, please." Jessica looked at him in amazement and started to push past him into the house.

"No—wait," he begged her. "The guy I did the internship with, he was really strange . . . otherworldly."

Jessica started to look angry.

"Look, he had a coffin in his house. I never saw him during the day, and while I was in New Orleans, there were several unexplained deaths right in our neighborhood. Deaths from people having all the blood sucked out of their bodies."

Her jaw set, her arms crossed over her chest, Jessica said, "So?"

"So the guy, Nicholas des Perdu, seemed obsessed with a picture I had of Elizabeth. He kept staring at it. It was even missing for a while."

"So?" Jessica repeated, looking over Tom's shoulder at the noisy and well-lit kitchen behind them.

"So now Nicholas is in town, hanging around SVU. I think I saw him, staring up at Elizabeth's window the night she almost jumped out. You yourself said she's acting weird. And three people have died around here in the last three days—because they had all the blood sucked out of them."

"Tom." Jessica looked patronizing. "Cut to the chase. What are you saying?"

Feeling as if he wanted to shake her, Tom exploded. "I'm saying I think Nicholas des Perdu is a serial killer—he thinks he's a vampire or something. I'm saying he's in town, I think he's obsessed with Elizabeth, and possibly has some kind of hold on her. I'm saying I want to know *where she is right now*!" he ended up screaming.

Jessica stared at him. Tom could see her mind working, see her trying to judge his story. Her head tilted thoughtfully to one side, her eyes gazed deeply into his. He felt as if he was going to start freaking out at any second.

"The roses," Jessica said, her forehead creasing into a frown.

"What roses? What are you talking about?" Tom snapped impatiently.

"Tonight our dorm room was filled—I mean totally filled—with roses. The card said, 'We'll be together tonight. N.' Elizabeth said she didn't know who N was. But maybe it was Nicholas. Maybe she was lying."

Tom stared at Jessica in horror. Part of him, he realized, had hoped that Jessica would have a boring, ordinary explanation for what was happening. Now, with a cold feeling of dread in his heart, his fears had been confirmed.

"Oh, no," he breathed.

Jessica gave a sharp nod. "Let's find her."

They pushed back into the party and together combed the place in three minutes flat. In the foyer they paused, each understanding that Elizabeth wasn't there. They would need a new plan fast.

Just as Tom was leaning down to yell in Jessica's ear over the loud music, the front door burst open. Denise Waters stood in front of them, her face pale, her pupils huge, tear streaks running down her face. Winston instantly rushed to her side.

"Denise, where have you been? What's happened?" he asked in a voice full of concern.

"Winston—you won't believe it," Denise said, her voice breaking. She caught sight of Jessica and held out her hand. "Jessica—something awful's happened."

Tom and Jessica hurried to Denise as other party-goers gathered around.

"Elizabeth?" Jessica asked urgently.

Denise shook her head. "No. Isn't Elizabeth here?"

"What happened, Denise?" Winston urged.

"It's Alison Quinn," Denise gasped, holding on to his arm. "We just took her to the hospital. Someone attacked her in her room—the new room," she added almost apologetically to Jessica. "It was horrible. There was blood everywhere. At the hospital they said that something—someone— had drained a lot of the blood from her body. Right in the Theta house." Denise's voice broke again, and fresh tears rolled down her face.

Jessica stared at her. "Alison Quinn? I—I saw someone approaching her window tonight, when she was in the room. I thought it was someone she knew."

"Oh, my gosh," Denise said. "You've got to go to the police."

"First we have to find Elizabeth," Tom said firmly, and Jessica nodded.

"Denise, I've got to go—we can't find Elizabeth. Is Alison—do you think she'll be all right?" For all the times that Jessica had complained bitterly about Alison, she had never *seriously* wished her dead.

Denise shook her head hopelessly. "They still don't know if she'll make it."

Then Tom was half dragging Jessica out the front door and into the damp, dark night.

Chapter
Ninteen

"I'm glad we're together." Nicholas's dark velvet voice surrounded Elizabeth like a sweet, heavy scent. It was still almost too good to be true, he thought, looking down at his beloved. His Lisette, who he had thought was lost forever, had been brought back to him. Now they would never be apart.

In just a few hours they would be at his home in New Orleans. Soon after that, Elizabeth would undergo the change necessary to keep them together forever, the change given to him by the mistress of pain. But he would be much more gentle with his beloved. For her it wouldn't hurt, wouldn't be shameful.

Lisette, you have never looked so beautiful. He gathered Elizabeth to him, feeling her slightness, as if she were a delicate bird. He had been powerless to save the original Lisette, powerless to bring her back from the dead. That had been a long time ago. He had power now, and he knew he never need fear losing her again.

It began to rain gently, and he turned on the Lotus's windshield wipers. They swept back and forth silently in a peaceful rhythm.

Dreamily she smiled up at him, leaning her blond head against his shoulder as he drove expertly through the streets surrounding Sweet Valley University.

"Where are we going, Nicholas?" she asked, her voice low and slightly husky.

"We're going home, my darling. First to New Orleans, and then to my family home outside of Paris."

"Oh, good," Elizabeth said softly. "I can't wait."

"Where first?" Jessica asked when she and Tom were outside. A chilly rain was starting to fall, but she hardly noticed it.

"You wait here—I'll check outside the house really quick," Tom commanded.

Jessica could only nod, staring through the dark night as Tom ran off. Inside she could hear the music, still pounding loudly.

Once Denise's news spread, the party would probably die down some. Probably, not definitely, Jessica acknowledged wryly. There were some serious good-time-havers in there.

Tom was back almost immediately, his dark hair glistening with drops of rain, his handsome face looking strained and intense. "There's no sign of her. What now?"

"The dorm?" Jessica suggested. "Maybe she went back there to change or something." She followed Tom as they ran to his car, only one of dozens of cars parked all over the dried dead lawn of the old house.

Soon they were buckled in and speeding toward the dorm. "You know, I saw her get into a car with a strange guy a few days ago. I asked her about it, but she said she was working on a story. I believed her. But what if it was him?"

Tom downshifted around a corner, his tires almost skidding on the wet pavement. "We'll find her," he said grimly. An unwanted memory came back to him as they plunged through the dark streets around Sweet Valley University.

He remembered Marielle approaching him with her coffee-dark eyes, remembered how powerless he had been when she had tried to seduce him. In the darkness of the car, he flushed in embarrassment. As much as he loved Elizabeth, as devoted as he was to her, Marielle had exerted some kind of weird control over him that had practically led him to go to bed with her.

And Marielle was only Nicholas's housekeeper. How powerful was the man himself? What kind of hold did he have over Elizabeth? The situation was becoming clearer to Tom, now that he had accepted the idea that Nicholas was in town and was with Elizabeth.

He thought he could understand her growing preoccupation, her distance, her withdrawal. If Nicholas had a hold on her the way that Marielle had almost had a hold on him . . . then Elizabeth was in much worse trouble than he'd feared.

"There's no light on," Jessica said as Tom screeched to a halt in front of Dickenson Hall. Leaving the car parked illegally, they jumped out, pushed through the doors, and pounded up the stairs toward Jessica and Elizabeth's room.

Elizabeth, what are you doing? Jessica wondered, fumbling with her room key. *Where are you?* Usually Elizabeth was the one who had to bail Jessica out of trouble. Now it was Jessica's turn.

"She was here," Tom said tersely, picking up the discarded witch costume from Elizabeth's neatly made bed.

Jessica was flinging clothes aside in Elizabeth's closet. "There's nothing missing," she said, turning to Tom. "Her suitcases are here. Maybe they just went for a ride? I don't know."

Tom leaned against Elizabeth's desk, his face looking older and more tired than Jessica had ever seen it. Jessica felt worried, impatient, and very

243

scared for Elizabeth. But for Tom's sake she had to keep it together enough to try to help him. Somehow she felt that they would find Elizabeth only if they worked as a team. After all, they were the two people who loved Elizabeth the most.

"I don't think he wants to kill her," Tom said slowly, pinching his bottom lip. "Or at least not right away. I got the impression that he was more obsessed with her. So he would probably want to get to know her. Now, if he has her, would he keep her here, or . . ."

Moving fast, Tom grabbed the phone and pulled a crumpled piece of paper out of his pocket. Jessica watched while he dialed a number. "Yes, this is Omega Airlines. I have a plane ticket here for one of your guests, a Mr. N. Ofthelost," Tom said briskly into the phone. "I'm going to messenger it over right away."

*Mr. Ofthe*what? Jessica wondered.

"He has?" Tom sounded surprised, and Jessica began to bounce up and down with tension. "I see. Well, maybe there's been some mix-up. I'll be on the lookout for him here, then."

Tom clicked the receiver into place. "What was that all about?" Jessica demanded.

"That was the Sweet Valley Grande," Tom explained. "I found out Nicholas was staying there under an assumed name. I thought—I was hoping that he had taken Elizabeth to his room," he added uncomfortably. "But they said he checked out a couple hours ago, and that he was headed to the airport. He must have got everything ready before he picked up Elizabeth from the party. I guess he's . . . maybe taking her to New Orleans."

"Call the airport," Jessica said immediately. "Tell them there's a bomb on the plane to New Orleans."

Tom grinned. "That's not a bad idea," he said. "Except that they'll trace the call, put us in jail, and then we really won't be able to go after Elizabeth."

"Go after her? To New Orleans?" Jessica said.

"That's right," Tom said grimly. "You got any better ideas?"

After thinking for a moment, Jessica pulled out her small designer carry-on suitcase and began throwing clothes into it. "You call for tickets," she ordered. "Get us on the next flight out."

"Ladies and gentlemen, the weather in New Orleans is a balmy seventy-three degrees as we approach Moisant International Airport," the flight attendant said. "Local time is five-oh-three."

Elizabeth turned to Nicholas, who was sitting in the aisle seat next to her, holding her hand. As usual, he took her breath away. Even just sitting next to him, touching him slightly, was enough to make her pulse pound and her breath come quicker. He was beautiful, he was intelligent and mature, he was the sexiest man she'd ever met. . . . She was the luckiest woman in the world to be sitting there beside him. "I've never been to New Orleans," she said. "I can't wait to see it."

"You're going to love it, my dear. It's one of the most beautiful cities in the world. You will be the main jewel in its crown."

Elizabeth smiled, drinking in the planes of his cheeks, the depth of his green eyes, the thick black wave of his hair. A fierce jolt of possessiveness rocked her. *He's mine. Mine always.*

Before they had left SVU, she had seen something, or thought of something, that had made her feel sad. It had been in her room, maybe on her desk. What had it been? A picture? A letter? She couldn't remember. It was unimportant, anyway. The only thing that mattered was that she was with Nicholas. They were together, and they would be together forever. It was what she wanted. For the first time she felt that she knew the power of being a woman, a woman who wanted to be with her man.

Once they got to New Orleans, she would leave her childhood behind forever and enter an exciting new world unlike anything she had ever known—a world of sensuality, of intimacy, a world where she lived for herself, and for Nicholas, and not for anyone else. It was going to be wonderful.

* * *

"What do you mean, sold out?" Tom's voice was rising with frustration.

"I'm sorry, sir," the ticket clerk said. "We had a special on all our red-eye flights to New Orleans, and they sold out quickly. The next available flight"—she punched some buttons on her computer keyboard—"is not until tomorrow, at eleven A.M. It will arrive in New Orleans at . . . about five twelve P.M., central standard time." She looked up hopefully. "Shall I book you on that? We have a few seats left."

Tom looked at Jessica, and Jessica looked back. It was two thirty in the morning, and the airport was completely deserted. Tom felt the cold helplessness of the early morning creep over him. Didn't these people realize this was a matter of life and death? Didn't they know that Elizabeth had been abducted by a madman? Or at least that was the working theory, Tom acknowledged bitterly. He had absolutely no proof, as the police had pointed out when he and Jessica had appealed for their help.

At Jessica's tense nod he turned back to the clerk. "Fine," he said wearily. "Give us two tickets on that flight."

Jessica hoisted her suitcase. "I'll go stake us out some rows of seats to sleep on. We've got a long wait ahead of us."

*   *   *

The sky was still a deep purple-black when the small airplane landed at the New Orleans airport. Elizabeth peered out of her clouded plastic window but could see nothing in the early-morning dark. Smiling, Nicholas reached down and smoothed her hair back from her face. Feeling excited, almost giddy, she stood up and followed Nicholas out of the plane, down the small ramp that led directly onto the runway.

At the bottom of the ramp, a pleasant-looking man was standing next to a long black limousine.

"My dear," Nicholas said, "this is Fortune, my right-hand man. Fortune, meet Lisette."

The man bowed deeply to her, looking into her eyes, and Elizabeth gave him a shy smile. She liked the new nickname that Nicholas had given her. She was starting a whole new life, like a beautiful, exotic moth emerging from its chrysalis. It seemed fitting that she had a new name, too.

It was warm and dark and safe inside the limo. The windows were smoked, but Elizabeth could dimly see the lighted billboards along the sides of the highway. The land was very flat. Between the backseat and the front, where Fortune sat, was a piece of thick glass that Nicholas raised with the touch of a button.

Once they had their privacy, Elizabeth snuggled closer to Nicholas. "I'm excited to see your house," she said. "It feels like I've been there already, as if I know what it looks like."

"I know you will feel at home there," Nicholas said, gathering her close. She could feel his cool breath on her face, her neck, and a shiver of delight went down her spine. "I've waited so long," he whispered against her skin.

A strong lassitude swept over Elizabeth, and she sighed and let her head fall back against the seat. This was what she was meant for—to be with Nicholas. She felt as if she had known him forever, as if their destinies were irrevocably intertwined. Her life before he entered it was already fading, hard to remember. There was only the future. There was only the two of them.

"Mmm." Gently his lips brushed her hair. Then Elizabeth was in his arms, and he was kissing her, and she was kissing him back, pulling him closer, feeling him against her. His mouth trailed an icy-hot ribbon of kisses down to her neck, and then she suddenly drew in a sharp, surprised breath.

"Here we are, my dear." Nicholas's voice sounded hazy in her ears, and Elizabeth struggled to wake up. Blearily she opened her eyes to find that the limo had stopped. It was difficult to see through the car's dark windows, but she thought she could make out the large outline of a white house in the distance.

Elizabeth blinked. *I must have fallen asleep,* she thought. The car door was open, and Nicholas was leaning in toward her. His smile in the night's darkness was welcoming and very distinct; his face was the only thing she could really see clearly. Everything else was lost in a sleepy haze. Unfolding her limbs, she managed to get out of the limo with Nicholas's help.

"I'm sorry I dozed off," she apologized, her voice sounding thick to her ears.

"It's quite all right, Lisette," Nicholas said kindly. "I know you couldn't help it. Welcome to your new home."

Elizabeth looked around. It was still nighttime, but she could sense the faint air of expectation that precedes the dawn. The limo was parked in the middle of a large, overgrown yard. The trees and bushes were so dense that she couldn't see more than five feet into them. Ahead of her was a white house, a plantation house of the kind you see in movies. In the reflection of the full, setting moon, the house seemed to glow with a whiteness that was tempered by time and by rain into a gentle paleness. Elizabeth wondered what it would look like in the daytime, with the southern sun beating on it.

"Come," Nicholas said, taking her arm. They went down a brick path that was overgrown with soft dark-green moss, and up onto the low brick porch. Two massive oak doors stood ajar, and Elizabeth looked curiously at the figures carved on them.

They stepped into the darkened foyer that stretched the length of the house. To the left was a massive, curving staircase that seemed to float away from Elizabeth as she watched it. She felt herself sway against Nicholas, and she giggled.

"It's beautiful here," she said, but she wasn't sure if she meant it or not. Right now it was mostly very dark, and everywhere there were long shadows reaching off into the distance.

When Nicholas moved to the staircase and held out his hand, Elizabeth drifted toward him. This was it. She had crossed the threshold of adulthood. For the first time in her life, she was ready to take the final step toward being a woman. Here she was, with the man she loved, and she was planning to stay with him forever. Everything she wanted, everything she needed, she could find with Nicholas. Life was beautiful, exciting, darkly thrilling. So why did she have that niggling feeling in the back of her mind, as though she had forgotten something?

She shrugged to herself. It wasn't important.

When Nicholas opened a door at the top of the stairs, Elizabeth followed him without hesitation. The room was large, and lit only by several candelabra burning tall white candles. It was a feminine room, with airy, delicate antique furniture, flowered carpets, flowing linen curtains. Tall French windows looked out onto the darkness of the night.

"This will be your room for now," Nicholas told her, watching her face.

"It's beautiful," Elizabeth breathed, gazing at the gleaming furniture, the paintings on the walls, the carved marble fireplace. It reminded her of another room, oddly enough, of an empty, dusty, decrepit room. But she had no idea where that was.

"And this is your bed," Nicholas said in a seductive voice. He pulled back the wide panels of lacy mosquito netting, showing her a high four-poster bed that looked amazingly inviting.

Feeling an uncharacteristic boldness, a heady daring that she hadn't known she was capable of, Elizabeth turned and met Nicholas's deep jade eyes. "Where will you sleep?"

A slight spark rewarded her question as he gazed back at her. His beautiful mouth curved into a pleased smile, and he took her hand and kissed it.

"Tonight I will sleep in my own . . . place," he answered her. "But it is the last night I'll sleep there alone."

Blushing, Elizabeth smiled and looked away.

"Now," Nicholas said, "you're very tired.

You've had a long night. Climb into bed and sleep deeply, and at dusk we'll be together again."

Dutifully Elizabeth kicked off her shoes and climbed up onto the high bed. She'd never been so tired in her whole life, she thought, as she rubbed a finger over a tender spot on her neck.

"Do you have to go?" she asked sleepily, her head sinking gratefully into the plump down pillow.

"Yes, my dear," Nicholas whispered, drawing his hand over her eyes. They fluttered shut—she simply couldn't stay awake any longer. "It's almost dawn—I must leave you. But I will see you again when the sun goes down. Good night, Lisette. Remember always that I love you."

"Mmm," Elizabeth murmured, already half-asleep. "I love you, too."

When he was satisfied that she was truly in a deep sleep, Nicholas pulled away from the bed and arranged the netting. Behind him, Marielle took several quick steps toward the candles and began pinching them out.

"What do you think?" Nicholas asked softly, watching Elizabeth's sleeping form.

"The likeness is uncanny," Marielle's husky voice said. She pulled the curtains firmly across the windows. "There. Now the sun will not wake her." She grinned through the dark room at Nicholas.

Together they left Elizabeth and shut the door behind them.

"It's more than a likeness," Nicholas insisted as they went downstairs. "She truly is Lisette's reincarnation. And now she has returned to join me in my world, as I once tried to join her in hers."

Marielle patted his shoulder comfortingly as they moved through the kitchen. "I'm glad you have found her, old friend."

Nicholas nodded briefly as she opened the basement door for him. "Watch over her," he commanded as he slipped silently down the musty stairs. At the bottom of the stairs he checked his watch—only minutes till sunrise. He had cut it close. A sense of jubilation came over him as he ran one pale, long-fingered hand down the edge of the pretty, feminine white coffin that stood next to his own. He had ordered it especially for Lisette—he hoped she liked it. She would look amazingly beautiful lying on the pale-blue silk.

Then he opened his own coffin lid and wearily lay himself down among the tufted gray fabric. Everything had gone perfectly, he congratulated himself. Now Lisette was with him. He would never again feel that aching sense of loneliness, of loss, that he had felt all these many years. His life was good again, full of meaning, full of purpose.

Starting tonight, he and Lisette could explore the world together.

Just as the sun's faintest pale-pink fingers began to reach over the far-off curved horizon, Nicholas lowered the lid of his coffin and prepared to go to sleep.

Chapter
Twenty

_____

"It's all my fault," Tom muttered as the flight attendant took away their plastic lunch trays.

Jessica felt a tiny bit of irritation. If it was anyone's fault, it was hers—she was Elizabeth's twin. "How's that?" she said coolly, glancing out the airplane window toward the blinding white clouds below them.

"I should have known something was wrong. I should have made her tell me."

Out of the corner of her eye Jessica could see that Tom was methodically shredding his paper napkin into little bits.

"I see. You should have automatically assumed that Elizabeth didn't know her own mind, and that you knew better than she did," Jessica said disdainfully. "Even though she said nothing was wrong, you should have discounted her feelings. It was silly of

256

you even to give her the benefit of the doubt. After all, she's just a dumb blonde, and you're a big man."

"You know I don't think she's a dumb blonde!" Tom snapped. "But let me get this straight. You're saying it's better that I respect her feelings and let her get killed than to rely on my knowledge of her personality and force her to admit something is wrong! Is that how you feel?"

"I don't know how I feel," Jessica admitted in an angry whisper. "I guess I should have been more suspicious, too. But you can't go around living people's lives for them." Feeling close to tears, Jessica turned her head away and leaned it against the cold thick plastic of her window. Arguing with Tom was pointless. Part of her knew they were bickering only because they were so worried about Elizabeth. They both felt guilty and helpless. *Oh, Lizzie. I've let you down.*

Several minutes went by as they sat in tense silence. Below them the sun shone so brightly on the thick cloud cover that it hurt Jessica's eyes to look at it.

"The cops in New Orleans were unimpressed with my story," Tom said finally, breaking the silence.

"That's right," Jessica said. "I'd almost forgotten you called them this morning. Exactly what did they say?" She sat up and brushed her hand across her eyes.

Tom shrugged, his face tight. "They weren't

about to go search Nicholas des Perdu's house just on my say-so. He's famous, he's rich, they think he's a leading citizen. And I'm a nobody. They warned me about harassment."

"We don't need them, anyway," Jessica said, her eyes narrowing. "The two of us can do it." She met Tom's eyes, and he nodded, smiling faintly. They were a team. She only hoped they weren't too late.

"Can't you go any faster?" Tom urged the taxi driver, leaning over the front seat.

"We're already doing seventy, mister," the man said lazily. "What's the rush?"

"Just hurry," Tom said.

In the backseat he and Jessica sat stiffly. He felt exhausted from the long night of worry, the day spent in a stuffy airplane, and now this interminable taxi ride from the airport to the French Quarter. The sun was low on the horizon; shadows were lengthening, the clouds in the sky were burned orange and pink along their bottom edges. Tom could feel sweat trickle down his back, and he rolled down his window.

"I wonder how Alison Quinn is," Jessica said softly as she wrestled her hair into a braid to prevent it from being blown into snarls by the wind.

Tom thought for a second. "If she was still alive after the attack, she has a chance."

"Yeah. I just can't believe I was fighting with her

over that room." Jessica's blue-green eyes looked shiny. "I said . . . I said I wished she would drop dead. And you know what else? I was so furious that she'd locked me out of that room. But if she hadn't, *I* would have been in there. That could have been me. And . . . I'm glad it wasn't. Is that terrible?"

"Jessica, of course you're glad that you're still OK. That's only human. Your fight with Alison had nothing to do with Nicholas attacking her. It isn't your fault. Don't start thinking like that."

"The worst part is that I was thinking about Elizabeth while we were waiting in the airport. And I prayed that as long as we got Elizabeth back, I didn't care what happened to Alison." She sniffled and put her hands over her face.

"Shh, shh," Tom said, putting his arm around Jessica and awkwardly patting her shoulder. "Don't worry about it. We're both thinking things like that. It's because we love Elizabeth so much. You're not an awful person just because you want your sister to live. None of this is your fault. We're going to find Elizabeth, and it'll be OK. Now, we don't know what we're going to face, and I need you to hold together."

Jessica nodded, sniffled again, and sat up straighter.

"Good," Tom praised her. "It won't be long now."

*   *   *

It took all of Elizabeth's will to force her eyes open. She was supremely comfortable, lying in bed, and felt as if she could stay there for another week. But a dim light fell across her eyelids, making her unhappily aware that it was probably getting late, and she had to get up if she wanted to make her first class.

The first thing she saw when she pried open her eyelids was a bed canopy, right above her. It was lined with pale-yellow silk, gathered tightly, and knotted in the middle. A glance around showed her that she was surrounded by a fine lace netting. Nothing about the bed looked familiar.

What's going on? Where am I? Sitting up, Elizabeth looked down at her clothes. A blue button-down shirt, white jeans, socks. Regular clothes.

A thin gray shaft of light was permeating the lace curtain. Elizabeth pushed the netting aside and slid off the high bed. She was in a beautiful, old-fashioned room. Walking to the window, she opened the heavy drapes and looked out. All she saw was an overgrown yard, and the low tops of pink stucco buildings beyond a tall brick wall. She wasn't wearing a watch, but judging from the sun, it was late afternoon, almost sunset.

Where am I?

She shook her head. It felt thick and achy, as though it were filled with soggy cotton balls. Was she sick?

Nicholas. Dim memories started filtering through her brain. A plane ride in the night? Oh, no. She was in New Orleans. She had left Sweet Valley and come to New Orleans with Nicholas des Perdu. What had she been thinking?

A wave of dizziness and nausea came over her, and she put her hand to her head. A wet washcloth—something to drink. She had to figure out what to do. Gingerly she opened the door to her room, but no one came, and the house felt empty and still around her. She had to find Nicholas and see what was going on.

The room next to hers was a charming, old-fashioned bathroom, and she splashed cold water onto her face. She wanted to check her appearance—she was sure she looked like death—but there were no mirrors anywhere.

Next to the bathroom was another bedroom, but it was dark and masculine compared to hers. It, too, was filled with beautiful antiques, and Elizabeth took a moment to trace the marble-topped dressing table with her finger. A tiny piece of paper was sticking out of its drawer. Feeling guilty, Elizabeth pulled the drawer open and looked at it. It was a torn-out page of notebook paper, covered with handwritten notes.

The black handwriting looked strangely familiar, and Elizabeth frowned, wondering where she had seen it before. When the realization hit her, it was as if someone had thrown a bucket of ice water over her head.

Tom.

These were Tom's notes, left behind when he had finished his internship with Nicholas. *What am I doing here? Nicholas wanted to talk about Tom's award. . . .*

Feeling even more bizarre, Elizabeth stuck the paper back into the drawer and left the room. Thinking about Tom made her want to cry. She didn't belong with Nicholas—it was Tom she loved. How could she have betrayed him this way? What was wrong with her? Maybe she was going crazy.

But no matter what, she had to find Nicholas and explain that the whole thing had been a horrible mistake. She had to get back to Sweet Valley right away. If Tom hated her, she wouldn't blame him. There was no explanation she could offer him.

At the end of the hall a large, beautiful staircase curved along one wall. Trying to steel herself to tell Nicholas that she had to leave immediately, Elizabeth padded downstairs.

But the first floor seemed just as deserted. The sun was going down now, but no one had turned on any lights. The house seemed dark and strangely quiet. The first room that Elizabeth went into was a large double parlor. In the increasingly dim light, Elizabeth could make out a black grand piano in one corner. She flicked on a lamp. Nearby was a large painting on an easel, covered with a square of pink silk moire.

Again feeling as if she was snooping, Elizabeth carefully lifted the silk covering.

What in the world?

It was a portrait. Elizabeth stared at it uncomprehendingly, then stepped back a few paces. The painting looked as if it had been created hundreds of years ago, judging by the clothes and jewelry the subject was wearing, and the way her blond hair was styled. But there was no way the portrait could be that old, Elizabeth decided uneasily. Because it was of her. She was the woman in the painting—it was her face looking wistfully out of the frame, her eyes that seemed to follow Elizabeth wherever she looked. It was Elizabeth, wearing a wedding gown hundreds of years old.

How totally creepy. Where did Nicholas get this, and why?

For the first time since she had woken in a strange room in a strange house in a strange city, Elizabeth felt afraid.

Sunset. Although it was completely black inside his coffin, Nicholas was aware of the exact moment the burning sun finally sank below the watery horizon. His eyes opened, and his fingers rubbed against the familiar silk. He was home again. When he smiled, his beautiful, finely carved mouth revealed perfect, shiny teeth. *Lisette*. It was time.

She was in the parlor when he found her, standing in front of her portrait. One lamp was lit, highlighting her golden, shining hair.

"The image does not do justice to the reality," he murmured, kissing her cheek. Lisette stared up at him with troubled eyes.

"Nicholas," she began in the gentle voice he knew and loved.

"I know what the problem is, darling," he interrupted lovingly. "You don't feel like yourself. But look what I have here. I've saved it for you all these years."

Lisette stared at the dress in his hands, then looked at her portrait. "It's the same dress," she whispered.

"Yes, my love. Now, please put it on, for my sake. I know you'll feel better once you do. And then we can be joined forever, just as we planned." He ran his fingers down the golden fall of her hair, allowing himself the luxury of enjoying its soft texture. Lisette slowly took the dress from him and went out of the parlor and up the stairs.

As soon as she was gone, Marielle came into the parlor.

"Fortune is taking me hunting in some of the little fishing villages down by Grande Isle," she said, adjusting her black turtleneck. "Good luck with Lisette."

"Luck is not necessary at this point," Nicholas said smugly. "Lisette is mine forever. Have a good time with Fortune."

"Oh, I will. Believe me." Marielle snapped her teeth at him coquettishly.

In her room upstairs Elizabeth stood in front of the dresser, trembling. It was obvious now that *she* wasn't the crazy one. It was Nicholas. Looking into his brightly burning green eyes, she had seen only madness—madness and a fierce need to believe she was this Lisette person, whoever she was.

Instinctively Elizabeth knew she had to go along with Nicholas for the moment, at least until she came up with a plan, or until a way to escape presented itself. But it would be much easier to think, to plan, if she didn't still feel so tired and out of it.

Keep it together, Elizabeth, she warned herself, quickly getting into the dress. *You are your only hope.* The knowledge filled her with a quick despair that she squashed immediately.

Taking a deep breath, Elizabeth left her room to go downstairs. In the hallway a massive black telephone that looked at least fifty years old caught her eye. She hadn't noticed it before, but now she grabbed it in desperation and dialed the first number that popped into her head: Tom's.

A cool, gentle hand relieved her of the receiver's

weight, and Elizabeth turned to look into Nicholas's mesmerizing stare.

"Come, my darling," he said, replacing the phone on the hook. "The sooner we begin, the sooner we can start our lives together."

"Begin what?" Elizabeth asked warily as Nicholas led her back into her room. A cold feeling of dread made her stomach knot up.

"Begin the process of our joining," Nicholas said, striking a match and lighting several candles on the mantel and the dresser. "As I told you. After tonight we'll never be parted again."

Although Elizabeth tried to look away, his gaze held hers compellingly. Once again she realized how beautiful he was, how finely sculpted his features were. Maybe he didn't mean her harm, after all. Maybe she was just being silly, wanting to leave him. His hand was trailing up her arm, gathering her close to him, and then Elizabeth remembered that she really should be trying to escape. But suddenly it seemed like so much trouble . . . even thinking about it was difficult. Her thoughts, her cares, her worries, seemed to be fluttering away like startled birds, flying off into the night.

Nicholas's mouth on hers was painfully familiar, hauntingly seductive. She couldn't help responding to the pressure of his lips, the insistent stroking of his hands on her back. The kiss went on, deeper and deeper until Elizabeth felt dizzy. Her head was spinning, she was floating mindlessly. Her eyes fluttered shut and the world disappeared, leaving her aware only of the steady beating of her heart.

When his lips began to trail a line of icy fire down her neck, Elizabeth felt an electric shock run through her. There was a tender spot on her neck—she had woken up with it. Now she felt his mouth, burning hot, press against it. Her hands were clutching his shoulders; she dimly sensed she would fall without him. Then she felt an increasingly sharp pressure against her skin. . . .

When Nicholas actually bit her, the whole picture suddenly snapped into focus for Elizabeth. Her body was growing cold, her heart was pounding fuzzily in her brain. Nicholas's sharp teeth had pierced her flesh, leaving two fine holes. It was enough. Summoning every ounce of her strength and willpower, Elizabeth pushed Nicholas away and screamed as loud as she could. Reeling almost drunkenly, she broke away from him and fell to one side, trying to get some distance between them. One hand knocked over a candle, and it fell onto the Persian carpet with a splash of tallow.

Silently Nicholas came toward her, his green eyes glowing ominously as he licked his reddened lips. Elizabeth stumbled over a chair, then bolted out the door to careen down the hall. His shadow loomed large behind her, and she screamed again.

Chapter
Twenty-one

Tom's dark eyes widened, and Jessica's head snapped back to stare at him in horror. They were on the low brick porch outside of Nicholas's house, having laboriously climbed the slick and moldy brick wall to get into the estate.

"That's Elizabeth!" Tom cried, pounding on the front door. Frantically he looked for a way to get in. Then he and Jessica, acting on an unspoken command, ran around the side of the house. There was a small brick patio there, with several pieces of heavy white wrought-iron furniture.

Without thinking, Tom grabbed a chair and slammed it into a tall French door, shattering the wooden frame and exploding the glass panes.

Then he and Jessica leaped through the opening, ignoring the dangling, razor-sharp shards that hung around the frame.

* * *

The house was dark and unfamiliar, and Elizabeth had crashed into door frames and furniture too many times to count. Always Nicholas was right behind her, moving with fast, silent ease through his domain, laughing at her pathetic attempt to escape.

"Come, Lisette, my darling. Enough games. You know we were meant to be together. Why else would you come back?"

Almost sobbing with terror, Elizabeth flung herself into yet another room and slammed the door. There was no place to hide, no place for her to go. If only she could get outside . . . From far off in the distance she heard the sound of breaking glass, but just then Nicholas swooped silently into the room. His face was white and glowing except for the warm flush of pink in his cheeks. His cruel, beautiful mouth was carved into a determined smile, and then his hands were on her, catching her close to him.

With all her strength Elizabeth beat against him, screaming. But he subdued her as easily as a dragonfly. Her screams died in her throat as he bent her head back over his arm and sank his teeth into her once again.

"Drop her!" Tom shouted, bursting into the room. Leaving Jessica downstairs, he had thundered up the wooden staircase, following the sound of Elizabeth's cries.

Now Nicholas looked up in surprise, his handsome face contorting into a grotesque mask of rage and thwarted desire. Gently he laid Elizabeth down on a damask couch, then rose to his full height and faced Tom. He looked huge and terrible, not at all like the suave, cultured man Tom had known during his internship.

"I know all about you," Tom snarled, trying to quell the fear that was rising in his throat. For one instant he took his eyes off Nicholas to glance at Elizabeth. She was unconscious, but he thought he saw her chest move with a shallow indrawn breath.

"So help me, if you've really hurt her," Tom threatened, feeling an unstoppable anger washing over him. Adrenaline flooded his body, making him feel invincible.

Nicholas laughed then, moving toward Tom so fast, it was as if he flew there. Tom felt a stinging blow across his face and fell back hard against a chair, turning it over. His lip split open, and the tangy taste of blood filled his mouth. As Nicholas came toward him again, his face stretched in a horrifying, triumphant expression, Tom suddenly swirled the blood in his mouth and spit at him, trying to gain time to make it out the door.

It worked, but only for an instant. Nicholas

reeled back in surprise, wiping the bloody spit out of his eyes. Then, with a low snarl, he raced after Tom toward the stairs.

Get him away from Elizabeth, was the only thing Tom had time to think before Nicholas lunged for him again, catching him with a mighty blow to the chest that left Tom gasping and grabbing the wall in support. As Nicholas moved in for another hit, Tom pulled his strength together and straightened up. He used all of his power to throw a punch at the stronger man.

Nicholas easily sidestepped it, still grinning, and Tom's fist crashed into the wall, causing him to grunt with shocked pain as his knuckles exploded.

Moving as slowly and as gracefully as a ballet dancer, Nicholas reached out and almost casually grabbed Tom's shirt, pushing him backward toward the stairs. With only the use of his left hand, Tom desperately tried to hold on to Nicholas. But it was no use. As if he were throwing away an empty bottle, Nicholas flung Tom down the wide staircase.

It wasn't until Tom was lying crumpled and breathless at the bottom that he realized two things—he was still alive, and he smelled something burning.

He tried to unfold his bruised and aching limbs, but his enemy was already there, hauling him to his feet, slamming him against the wall. He pulled back one delicate, long-fingered white hand and curled it into a fist that Tom knew would feel like white-hot iron. Tom drew in a deep breath, waiting for the blow, powerless to stop it.

"Hold it right there!" Jessica cried behind them. Tom had almost forgotten about her in the fight and his relief at finding Elizabeth alive.

Slowly Nicholas turned. Behind them stood Jessica, looking both furious and scared. She held a heavy candelabra and was swinging it like a baseball bat.

Tom felt Nicholas's hand slacken on his shirt, saw his fist lower slightly. His green eyes were open in shock, as if he couldn't believe what he was seeing.

"Let him go!" Jessica shouted, waving her candelabra threateningly.

"Lisette?" Nicholas's voice sounded confused.

Tom instantly ducked out of Nicholas's way and tried to motion to Jessica that he was going upstairs to get Elizabeth. Jessica nodded faintly, and Tom spun and started leaping up the stairs two at a time.

Feet don't fail me now. Oddly enough, it was the only thing Jessica could think at that moment. She knew Elizabeth must be upstairs, alive and all right, if they were lucky; she knew that Tom was getting beaten to a pulp by this tall pale guy in front of her; she knew that somewhere in this house, something was on fire. But all she could pray for at that moment was that her feet didn't collapse under her.

"Lisette?"

So this is Nicholas des Perdu, famous journalist, Jessica thought, licking her lips nervously as the man came closer. He was staring at her in confusion, as if she were a ghost. She hefted the candelabra higher.

Where are Tom and Elizabeth? I need time.

"Lisette?" Jessica asked, backing slowly down the hall. "Who's Lisette?"

"You're Lisette," Nicholas said in an aristocratic voice. "But why have you changed? Where's your wedding dress?"

OK, this guy's a few accessories short of an ensemble. Got it. However, even in the middle of everything Jessica could understand Elizabeth's attraction to him. He was one of the most handsome and charismatic guys she'd ever seen. If he had a tan, he'd be totally devastating.

"Um, my wedding dress," Jessica stalled, knowing that she had to play along with him. His green eyes looked deeply into hers, and he came closer. Her candelabra was getting heavier and suddenly seemed like a ludicrous weapon. "My wedding dress. Well, I decided to go with a more, you know, casual look."

Slowly Nicholas started to advance on her. She had seen what he had done to Tom. She knew he was dangerous. He just didn't *seem* that dangerous right *now*. He was so amazingly attractive, even with that bloody stain on the collar of his shirt . . . Jessica's candelabra floated gently to the ground.

Upstairs Elizabeth's eyes fluttered open when Tom scooped her up into his arms. She looked pale, and there were faint blue smudges under her eyes. With horror Tom noticed the two red-rimmed puncture wounds on her neck.

"Tom," Elizabeth whispered. "Help me."

"I will, Liz," he promised hoarsely. "We have to get you out of here." In the hallway, flames were licking around the door frame of the next room. The air was thick and heavy with choking smoke. Leaning heavily on Tom's arm, Elizabeth managed to make it to the stairs just as a large fire-ball broke free and rolled down the hallway toward them. The fire was consuming everything: the carpets, the curtains—even the oil paintings on the walls were exploding into popping bursts of combustion.

Clumsily they made it downstairs, and with a sinking feeling Tom noticed that Jessica and Nicholas were nowhere to be seen in the foyer. But he pulled Elizabeth toward the front door, both of them starting to gag on the thick smoke.

As fast as he could, he pushed her out the front door and away from the house to the lawn. As soon as he let go of her, she fainted, sinking gracefully onto the grass, with her antique dress folding beneath her.

When Tom looked back at the house, he saw the whole upstairs wreathed in tall flames that filled the black night sky, lighting it with feathery plumes of yellow and orange. Even the first-story windows were glowing faintly. And Jessica was inside.

"You're beautiful," Nicholas whispered, leading Jessica to the sofa in the large front parlor.

Tell me something I don't know, Jessica thought. But inside she felt as if she were falling into deep green pools of soothing water. What a relief it would be to sink into them forever, far away from this acrid burning in her throat, away from the flying flecks of fine black ash swirling around her eyes.

Nicholas's cool hands were smoothing her shoulders, brushing her face. Jessica stared up at him, willing him to continue. She was breathless with anticipation.

"Nicholas," she whispered as his head slowly lowered for a kiss.

In the next instant Nicholas was clubbed heavily from behind, and his head slammed down against the sofa back. With an angry roar he leaped up, and Jessica saw Tom standing there, breathing hard, a bloodied marble urn in his hands.

"Jessica! Get out!" he screamed.

But Jessica felt unable to move. Nicholas, his face a terrible study of rage and fury, started to move toward Tom as she watched. With one final heave Tom flung the urn at Nicholas, catching him in the chest and knocking him backward several feet.

Then, as if in a dream, Jessica felt Tom grab her roughly around the waist, haul her up, and jump with her through a closed window. In a terrifying explosion of wood and glass, Jessica felt herself propelled from a world of fear and flames and seduction into a world of blessedly cool night air.

When she saw Elizabeth, she collapsed next to her. Then she grabbed her twin's hand and passed out.

As if new life had been breathed into her lungs, Elizabeth opened her eyes. Turning to the left, she saw Jessica, her face scratched, bloody, and streaked with soot. Jessica was holding her left hand tightly, and Elizabeth squeezed it. This was why she felt whole again—she was united with her twin, her other half. Jessica had saved her.

To the right was Tom, looking away from her toward the huge, ancient, beautiful house that was engulfed in flames. He was holding her right hand with his left one. His face was bruised and dirty, and one eye was swollen shut. Tom. Her beloved Tom. He had come after her. Together with Jessica, he had saved her life. A feeling of overwhelming love and gratitude swept through Elizabeth, and a single tear rolled down her face. Gently she reached out and stroked his cheek, and he turned toward her.

Their eyes met, dark ones looking into blue-green ones, and Elizabeth felt no need to speak.

In the next moment Jessica roused herself, and the three of them got stiffly to their feet. Whining sirens got closer and closer, and soon they could hear men with axes breaking through the rusted iron gates at the end of the driveway. The flames were so high and hot that Jessica, Tom, and Elizabeth backed away from the house, edging into the lush, overgrown tangle of oak trees, passion vines, and azalea shrubs.

Then the firemen finished breaking through the gates, and huge, noisy red trucks were grinding heavy wheels into the damp grass. As men started hauling canvas hoses toward the house, Elizabeth thought she saw a single raven-black shadow detach itself from the house and slide into the trees beyond. But when she looked again, it wasn't there.

Chapter
Twenty-two

Sweet southern-California sunshine flooded through the windows of Dickenson Hall and slanted across the pastel quilt on Elizabeth's bed. She stretched and yawned lazily, then absentmindedly scratched an itchy spot on her neck beneath the cotton scarf tied there.

Another beautiful day, filled with promise. Elizabeth sighed contentedly and snuggled beneath her quilt.

"OK, up and at 'em," Jessica's cheerful voice said as the door banged open and hit Elizabeth's closet.

Elizabeth smiled to herself.

"Look what I brought," Jessica said proudly, setting a cafeteria tray on Elizabeth's bed as Elizabeth scrambled to sit up and arrange her covers. "Broth, tea, and the mail. You got a new *Time* magazine."

"Hmm, this smells good," Elizabeth said appreciatively, taking the cover off the hot soup. "Any fun mail?"

Jessica was flipping through envelopes. "Catalog, catalog, fashion magazine for me, letter for you, bill, bill—oh, I'll take that one—catalog."

"Great, thanks," Elizabeth said, taking a sip of her hot tea. While Jessica started flicking through her magazine, Elizabeth took the opportunity to examine her sister. Almost all of the scratches on her arms and face had healed, and there wouldn't be any scars, thank goodness. Every once in a while a look of confusion would cross her face, but in general she was snapping back to business as usual. Elizabeth grinned to herself. Her twin was nothing if not resilient.

"Jess? Any news on Alison Quinn?" Elizabeth asked.

"Hmmm?" Jessica looked up. "Oh. Yeah. They say she'll be OK after a while. She needed a huge transfusion. They're keeping her in the hospital for at least another week."

"So who gets the room?" Elizabeth asked mischievously. "With her in the hospital, you have a clear shot, right?"

Jessica's face wrinkled into a frown of disgust. "Ugh. Who wants it? There's no way I could sleep in that room now. And come to think of it, it wasn't really *me*. No, I guess I better stay here for a while," she said firmly. "Especially since you still need me."

At Jessica's self-satisfied expression, Elizabeth couldn't help breaking into a chuckle.

Jessica trotted easily down the stairs of Dickenson Hall. Her heart was light, it was a beautiful day, and she was meeting Randy at the Coffee House in ten minutes. More important, Elizabeth seemed almost herself again. True, sometimes her face was haunted, as if she was recalling a wisp of memory better left forgotten, but in general she was recovering well. And she and Tom were back to being their usual revolting lovey-dovey selves, which was a good sign.

"Excuse me." Jessica was stopped by a white-uniformed delivery boy carrying a large green florist's box. "Do you know where I can find Elizabeth Wakefield?"

"Yeah," Jessica said cheerfully. "But I can take those to her. Where do I sign?"

The boy showed her, and Jessica scrawled her name. After he headed back down the stairs, Jessica turned to carry the flowers up to Elizabeth. No doubt they were from Tom Terrific, Jessica thought dryly.

But as she climbed the stairs to their floor, an odd feeling came over her. It wouldn't hurt to look. For Elizabeth's own good, of course. She tore off the ribbon and opened the box.

Nestled against tissue paper lay a dozen of the most beautiful roses Jessica had ever seen. Long-stemmed, bright-leaved, full buds on the brink of opening into massive, full-headed blooms. There was no card. Jessica regarded the roses for a moment, then calmly put the lid back on the box, tied the ribbon, and headed back downstairs.

Outside the dorm there was a trash Dumpster, and Jessica heaved the box inside without a second glance. Then, whistling, she headed for the short-cut through the quad that would take her to the Coffee House.

Inside the Dumpster the box burst open, and the roses spilled out. Eleven icy-white blooms slid down the pile of trash and mingled with old food, crumpled paper, and other assorted trash. A single blood-red rose rested on top of the huge pile of debris, its sweet scent mixing with the fetid smell of garbage.

Now that Jessica Wakefield has noticed Louis Miles, one of the most attractive guys she's ever seen, there's no way she's going to forget he's around. But when it turns out that Louis is a Sweet Valley University professor, will Jessica get into a relationship that's over her head? Find out in Sweet Valley University 15, Behind Closed Doors.

We hope you enjoyed reading this book. If you would like to receive further information about available titles in the Bantam series, just write to the following address, with your name and address:

Kim Prior
Bantam Books
61–63 Uxbridge Road
Ealing
London W5 5SA.

If you live in Australia or New Zealand and would like more information about the series, please write to:

Sally Porter
Transworld Publishers
(Australia) Pty Ltd
15–25 Helles Avenue
Moorebank
NSW 2170
AUSTRALIA

Kiri Martin
Transworld Publishers (NZ) Ltd
3 William Pickering Drive
Albany
Auckland
NEW ZEALAND